SLAVES OF THE SULTAN

BOOK
THE INCA...
OF WHIT...
Commander

Copyright Allan Aldiss

Bondage Books
http://www.bondage-books.com

PROLOGUE

Allan Aldiss has written many stories about life in make-believe harems. However, this one is different. It is about life in a real harem: the harem of almost the last of the Sultans of Turkey, who only a hundred years ago was the all-powerful Ruler of the still vast Ottoman Empire.

The organisation of this harem is well known and the vast, luxurious, building that housed it, the harem quarters of the Dolmabahçe Palace in Istanbul, has been restored to its former glory.

It was looking round this intriguing and relatively modern harem building that made Allan decide to write a story featuring some of the European girls, including two well educated young English girls, who might well have been secretly incarcerated in it.

The result is a well researched historical novel with erotic overtones - not a mere story of floggings and beatings, but very much a real story of subjugated white women. It is based on fact.

This then is an Allan Aldiss story with a difference.

Dramatis Personae

His Imperial Highness Abdul Hamid II - Sultan of Turkey and of the Ottoman Empire
His Highness the Kizlar Aghasi - The Chief Black Eunuch

Agha Selim - The Commander of the Syrian or Green Orta
Tulip - One of Agha Selim's assistant eunuchs
Agha Kasim - The Agha of the Gedekli
Agha Vazid - The Agha of the Innocent Virgins
Agha Ali - The Commander of the Balkan or Blue Orta
Agha Manju - The Agha of the Curved Bellies
Shu-shu - The Sultan's pet white eunuch dwarf
Agha Turki - The Commander of the Greek or Blue and White Orta
Madeleine - A French slavegirl, formerly a governess
Helene - A Greek slavegirl, married to a rebel
Jane Carmichael - An English slavegirl
Fazileh-hanum - A Turkish slave dealer
Helen Hamilton - A friend of Jane
Ayab Bey - Equerry to the His Imperial Highness

Historical Background

Before the First World War the Ottoman Empire was a police state with a vast network of spies, stretching from the Caucasian Mountains to the Sahara Desert and from the Balkans to the Red Sea. Sultan Abdul Hamid II was revered by Moslems as the Padishah, the All-Highest, the Shadow of Allah on Earth. But he was known in Europe, and among his many Christian subjects, as Abdul the Damned.

Like many dictators he was obsessed with fear of assassination, particularly by members of the large and oppressed Christian provinces of the Empire. He only felt really safe in the harem quarters of his two modern palaces: the Dolmabahcheh (modern Turkish spelling: Dolmabahçe) on the edge of the Bosphorus, and the Yildiz (modern spelling: Yıldız) set in a park on a hill above.

These harems held his collection of white concubines, mainly Christians, who were kept cowed and constantly at his disposal by his black eunuchs. Their names quite unknown outside the walls of the harem. So were those of the four Kadins, the Sultan's favourites and often the mothers of his sons.

For centuries the Sultans had never married. Thus, like all the earlier Turkish Sultans, Abdul Hamid II was the product of a union between a Sultan and a slave woman. His father was the then twenty year old Sultan Abdul Mejid. His mother was a blond Circassian slavegirl, Pirimujgan, who had first come to the Sultan's notice as a dancing girl in the harem of his brother-in-law, a Pasha.

His sister, noticing her brother's interest in the girl, had given her to him as a present for the Moslem festival of Eid. Pirimujgan was now dead, her brief period of glory as the Valideh Sultana, the mother of the Sultan, was over - and the dreaded Kizlar Aghasi ruled the harem alone.

Abdul Hamid's grandfather was the great reforming Sultan Mahmud II, who had finally broken the power of the Janissaries, the elite corps of white soldiers seized as boys from the Christian provinces of the Empire and raised as fanatical Moslems.

A Sultan, of course, never publicly acknowledged the identity of his women. But it was generally accepted that that Mahmud's mother had been an aristocratic French slavegirl: Aimée du Bucq de Rivéry, a cousin of the Empress Josephine, the first wife of Napoleon.

Aimée had been captured by Barbary Corsairs whilst returning to her parents in France from a convent in Martinique in the Caribbean. The corsairs took her to the Bey of Algiers, who was so struck by the girl's beauty that he sent her a present to Sultan Abdul Hamid I, who promptly incarcerated her in his harem.

Chapter 1 - The Sultan Relaxes

It was a warm Spring evening in Constantinople just a hundred years ago. The Sultan was sitting back in his favourite armchair in the large villa that housed his harem in the park-like complex of the Yildiz Palace. He was relaxing after a busy day, listening to the pretty woman kneeling at his feet. She was reading him a salacious French novel.

It made a change from the usual displays of half naked dancing girls that the eunuch commanders of the various Ortas or brigades, into which his concubines were divided, vied with each to put on to arouse their Master's jaded libido.

The Sultan, a slight saturnine figure with a prominent hook nose over a long moustache and the piercing eyes of a ruthless voluptuary, smiled as he listened to the young woman's voice. Glad to be out of his gold encrusted uniform, he was relaxing in a loose silken robe.

Like all educated Turks, he was fluent in French; how delightful it now was to have a well educated, if reluctant, French slavegirl to read him the arousing story.

But the Sultan's real joy came from actually owning this beautiful Frenchwoman, whom he had allowed to keep her name: Madeleine. A feeling of power surged through his loins as he looked down at this once free European woman, now kept helpless, locked up in his harem, isolated from the sight of other men.

Through the elaborately barred window he looked out onto the well tended park and beyond it down onto the vivid blue of the Bosphorus, and up onto the green hills beyond. It all made a beautiful sight.

An equally beautiful sight was the twenty eight year old woman herself. Tall, with dark hair, flashing eyes and a good figure, she was despite her French nationality wearing the green coloured harem dress of a slavegirl of the Syrian Orta, which was largely made up of Christian Lebanese girls. However, she was now loaned to Agha Kasim's team of Gedekli - a dozen of the most beautiful young virgins, often still uncircumcised, in his harem. These were mainly blond girls from the Caucasus and were the Sultan's specially trained maids-in-waiting, or body servants.

The Sultan smiled as he remembered his delight when the Agha Selim, the Commander of the Syrian Orta who had bought her, had told him that thanks to her strict convent up-bringing she was still a virgin. Normally she would have been put into the Court of Innocent Virgins, her beauty lips carefully sewn up to preserve her virginity. And to preserve innocence she would have been kept isolated from the other harem slavegirls who would have had already encountered the Imperial manhood.

Here, deliberately kept untrained in the arts of love, she would have been kept under the supervision of Agha Vazid with half a dozen other virgins from different Ortas - but with one thing in common: none of them would have even seen an erect manhood. They provided a pool of beautiful and innocent virgins, each awaiting deflowering by the Sultan.

They made an interesting change from the well trained concubines of the various Ortas. The Sultan would periodically amuse himself by looking down at them from behind a lattice screen as he discussed with the Kizlar Aghasi which was ready for plucking

- or rather for her virginity to be offered up to him as she lay chained, helpless and horrified on his bed.

Then, after deflowering, she would have joined the girls of her Orta. Thus she would have had no opportunity to tell her still innocent previous companions what had happened to her - and what awaited them.

However, as this Frenchwoman was rather older than the run of his innocent virgins, he had decided as a rather erotic joke to incorporate her temporarily into his other team of virgins: the Gedekli. These virgins, sensuously half naked, with their beauty lips carefully sewn up and sealed with the Imperial seal, served in the Sultan's private apartments as his Maids of Honour. Here they were responsible under their experienced eunuch overseer for dressing and bathing the Sultan, for cleaning him after he made love or relieved himself. They washed his clothes, served his food and coffee, ritually washed him before the frequent regular Moslem prayers - and even, sometimes, aroused him with their fingers and tongues before he enjoyed one or more of his concubines, or took a virgin from the Court of Innocent Virgins.

They were also responsible for bringing him refreshments when he was enjoying one or more of his concubines and for attending on him by day or by night whenever he answered a call of nature.

The Gedekli might still be uncircumcised, but their beauty lips were also kept carefully sewn up by Kasim, a young eunuch Agha in charge of the Gedekli, to keep them pure and unable to masturbate. Kasim had only recently been promoted to Agha, but like his colleague, the Agha of the Innocent Virgins, he knew all about the naughty tricks that young uncircumcised white girls could get up to.

The Sultan smiled as he remembered how for the first time, Madeleine, her breasts held close together by their nipple chain and with her beauty lips carefully sewn up and sealed with the Imperial seal, had come running to his call to dress him for yet another audience with the French bankers.

He recalled how Kasim had then used his long whippy cane to make the shocked and innocent young Frenchwoman kneel down at his feet and, for the first time, reach up degradingly to hold the Imperial manhood in one hand, as he relieved himself into the jar she was humiliatingly holding in her other hand. Then, even more horrified, she had been made to lick him dry and later to attend on his further even more intimate ablutions, washing him clean with her fingers in the Turkish manner.

Perhaps even more satisfying had been when he had told her that he was about to see a group of her countrymen. He remembered how she had begged him in vain to give them a message for the grieving nuns in her former convent back in France.

'Freedom for you may for the moment seems very close,' he had angrily told her, 'but it in fact it is as far off as ever. You're going to remain here hidden in my harem as a slave forever. Understand?'

With a sob of despair that had delighted the Sultan, the woman had nodded.

The Sultan reminisced over how this Frenchwoman came to be in the Syrian Orta. Her parents had died and she had stayed on at her convent school in France as a teacher. Wanting to resist the constant pressure from the nuns to take the veil, she had accepted the chance of going as Governess to a rich Greek family in Beirut. After five happy years there, she had saved up enough money to return to France and, now with good-sized dowry behind her, to find a handsome husband.

But fate had intervened.

On the Turkish passenger ship to Constantinople, from where she was going to take a ship to Marseilles, she had been spotted by a scout from a leading firm of white slavers. Such a pretty and rare bird, he had decided, would be wasted returning to France to be Governess in a Christian household when she could be kept caged in Turkey in the harem of a good Moslem.

He became even more determined to get his hands on her when it became increasingly clear on the voyage that she was a well-educated and intelligent woman. A lusty Turk would enjoy bending such a woman to his desires all the more. Moreover, once locked up in his harem, his black eunuchs would of course make sure that she now dedicated herself to his pleasure with no thought of her own. The slaver had therefore bribed the Captain to issue a death certificate, stating that the girl had fallen overboard and been drowned the night before they arrived.

The slaver was a close contact of Agha Selim, the Commander of the Syrian Orta of the Imperial Harem. As she had been on her way back from Syria, he had offered her to him. Sensing a highly profitable opportunity and a way of getting one up on his great rivals, Agha Ali, the Commander of the Balkan Orta, Selim had snapped her up - despite her high price as a rare French slave. However, the dark haired young woman had proved to be pouting and self opinionated and it had taken young Agha Kasim several canings to break her into slavery and into her new degrading duties. Clearly she had also resented being supervised by a eunuch younger than herself.

Even now, looking down at her, the Sultan noted how her green coloured transparent silken pantaloons, through which gleamed her long legs, also scarcely hid the marks of a recent caning on her soft plump bottom - a sign that she had failed to treat her eunuch overseer with the instant obedience and proper respect that he expected from the young virgins under his control.

Kneeling up with her knees respectfully parted, her green cutaway harem pantaloons disclosed as with all the Gedekli the laces of her carefully sewn up beauty lips with the Imperial seal hanging down between her legs. The Sultan smiled secretively. Although she did not yet know it, those laces were due to be cut later that night to enable him, after she had been well oiled, to take her virginity - she would then, of course, have to leave the virginal Gedekli and rejoin Agha Selim's Syrian Orta.

A similar green coloured and embroidered bolero discreetly disclosed her firm breasts. A short light chain joined rings through her nipples, holding her breasts close together to give the cleavage that the eunuchs like to see on a white slavegirl. It was, moreover, a cleavage that served a useful purpose - forming, when the Sultan's fancy took him, a tight cushion for his throbbing manhood.

Round her neck was locked a collar of well polished steel. A lead had been fastened to the back. This lead was held by Tulip, a young eunuch overseer from her parent Orta, standing behind her. Each of the senior eunuchs in charge of an Orta had several junior eunuchs on their staff, often mere youths. To these they would delegate control, supervision and training of individual young women, or groups of women.

Like all the other eunuchs of the Imperial Harem, Tulip was proudly wearing a red fez on his head and was dressed in the Stambouline, a long black double-breasted morning coat, black trousers, stiff upturned white collar and black tie, worn by officials of the Ottoman Empire. Except for his red fez and black face and hands, he might well have been a well-dressed young gentleman in Paris or London. It was a dress that deliberately contrasted incongruously with that of the half naked young white Frenchwoman whose lead he was holding - as, of course, did his jet black skin.

In Tulip's free hand he was also proudly holding, like a military officer's swagger stick and as a similar sign of his authority, a long whippy bamboo cane with a curved handle. It was a cane that he had learned, despite his small size, to administer well and painfully to the backsides of the grown-up girls in his charge.

Here the cane was intended to ensure that the Frenchwoman showed proper respect to her Master. Tulip smiled as he saw that even whilst reading aloud, her eyes would occasionally dart back for a quick nervous glance at his cane. Yes, she was behaving well - as befitted a concubine of the Green Orta.

Moreover there was little chance of her in her nervousness disgracing him before the Sultan, for when collecting her earlier from Agha Kasim he had asked whether she had emptied herself properly that day. Glancing at his big wall chart on which all the Gedekli were listed, the Agha of the Gedekli had confirmed that she had.

Then attaching his lead to her collar, Tulip had taken her to the Gedekli's Turkish toilet. Standing over her, cane in hand, had made her spend a penny to his satisfaction. One could not be too careful, he reflected, with a new concubine.

In the left hand button hole of Tulip's Stambouline gleamed, like a military regimental cap badge, the green crest of the Syrian Orta of which he was an officer. In the right hand button hole, like the military badges of rank of officers, glittered a little golden Arabic numeral "3", which showed that he had been promoted to the rank of Three Stroke Eunuch. This was the first step up the ladder and gave him the right, without reference to his superiors, to administer three hard strokes of his cane to any girl in the Orta to which he was attached. If he showed zeal in disciplining the white women in his charge and in standing no nonsense from them, then he might expect to be promoted to the rank of a Seven or even Twelve Stroke Eunuch.

As a further security measure, the Frenchwoman's wrists were joined by a length of well-polished steel chain. Even in the secure and well-guarded harem quarters of the two palaces, behind the very high walls that surrounded the harems, Christian concubines were always kept manacled and on a lead in the presence of the Sultan - lest they be tempted to attack their hated Master.

Manacled with their hands held in front of their bodies, these Christian girls could not harm him even when, in accordance with the traditional Turkish manner of humiliating a Christian girl, they were made to kneel on all fours before their Master offering their raised washed-out and scented bottoms to be sodomised. Nevertheless, as a further precaution a young black overseer would as now be holding them by a lead attached to the rings at the back of their collars.

The manacle chains linking their wrists were long enough for an overseer to make the girls step over them when the Sultan indicated that for once he would like to penetrate one or more of them more normally or enjoy a little oral sex. In these cases, their young black overseer would make them lie on their backs in their Master's bed with their hips raised and their mouths open - as this Frenchwoman's would be later that evening, with her hands safely held chained behind her back, until the Sultan ordered her overseer otherwise.

These precautions were all signs of the Sultan's almost paranoid fear of being assassinated.

The Sultan felt a flash of anger as he remembered how that very afternoon, he had had to listen to a delegation of French bankers droning on about his profligacy and the need for retrenchment - just as the infuriating British Ambassador was also wont to do. But, listening to the Frenchmen, he had laughed to himself at the thought of how their faces would have dropped if he had told them that not only did he have an educated countrywoman of theirs secretly locked up in his harem, but that, unknown to her, he had told his eunuchs to get the woman ready to have her virginity taken later that very night.

If only, he thought, he had been able to do the same when next time the British Ambassador had had the effrontery to lecture him on the size of his harem and the need to abolish slavery. But the day would come...

The woman's voice stopped. Then reluctantly keeping her eyes respectfully lowered in the presence of the Commander of the Faithful, she reported: 'My Master, Sire, that is the end of the chapter.'

There was a rattling sound from her manacles as she humbly lowered her head to the floor, flinging her shiny long hair forward between her manacled hands. She had obviously been well trained by the eunuchs in charge of the Greek Orta.

Her long white back gleamed under its thin silken coverings and her slender waist made a vivid contrast with her raised bottom and swelling hips. Once again through her transparent harem trousers could be seen, across the cheeks, the fresh marks of the cane - testimony to the strict discipline of Kasim, the Agha of the Gedekli.

'Tulip!' said the Sultan, addressing the eunuch youth standing behind the kneeling woman and holding her by her degrading dog lead, for it was usual to give young eunuchs the names of flowers.

It was a harem rule that the Master did not demean himself by giving orders directly to one of his slavegirls, but instead gave them through the eunuch who always accompanied a concubine in his presence.

Moreover if the eunuch commanding a girl's Orta thought that it was likely that the Sultan would then honour the Orta by using her for his pleasure, then he would send one of his younger eunuchs to take charge of her - for the Sultan, like most Turkish Masters, found it less restricting to enjoy a girl in the presence of a youth rather than an older eunuch. Despite their young age, these youthful eunuchs still enjoyed the rank of an officer to emphasise their ascendancy over the white concubines.

With his other hand, Tulip was holding the well polished black leather retaining straps of the muzzle that he had earlier slipped off the woman to allow her to read aloud. Normally new Christian concubines, even those in the team of Gedekli, were kept muzzled in the presence of the Sultan to prevent them from annoying the Sultan by importuning him for their freedom - quite apart from trying to bite him.

'Yes, Tulip,' continued the Sultan, speaking in Turkish. 'I think it is time for a little pleasuring.'

Chapter 2 - The Last Day of Term

Meanwhile back in England two close friends, Jane Carmichael and Helen Hamilton, both aged eighteen, were about to leave school forever. They had been sent to this convent boarding school as child orphans by their guardians when their parents had died of that scourge of the British Empire: cholera. Jane's parents had died in India and Helen's in South Africa.

Jane had grown into a tall, slender and pretty young woman, with a good figure, lovely long blond hair, soft blue and intelligent eyes and a fair "peaches and cream" complexion. She was a rather quiet, nervous girl. Helen, by contrast, had long dark hair and dark eyes. She had a bubbling personality and flashing eyes. Her figure was every bit as attractive as Jane's.

They were both thrilled to be wearing for the first time, not the loose pinafores of schoolgirls in the late Victorian era, but the stays, long skirts and blouses of fashionable young women which showed off their pretty slim and yet firm breasted figures.

Jane adored Helen and was dismayed at the prospect of them being split up. Jane was going to rejoin her horrible old guardian who, on her rare visits to his house, never failed to stress that he had to spend all the money her parents had left and some of his own on her education. She would be penniless, he had said, when she left school.

How lucky Helen had been, Jane thought wistfully, when her guardian had agreed to her accepting an invitation from another girl who was also leaving the school. Maria Mavroyeni lived in Constantinople where her father was a leading Greek banker. She had invited both Jane and Helen to come and stay with her family in their large modern house in Pera, the European quarter of Constantinople, overlooking the Golden Horn. What a wonderful chance to see the world, and perhaps find a rich husband!

By contrast Jane's guardian had simply dismissed the invitation out of hand, saying that her trust fund could not possibly afford to pay for such a thing.

Unknown to Helen, her guardian had been only too delighted to have Helen taken off his hands. The longer the better as far as he was concerned, for he was still salting away her inheritance. There was little of left now and he was dreading having to account to Helen, now that she was nearly of age, for what had happened to it all.

The two girls were sitting on a comfortable big sofa in a pavilion some way from the main house of the school - having slipped away there to say goodbye in peace and quiet. Hesitantly, Jane reached out and touched Helen's hand.

'Oh, how I'm going to miss you,' she murmured.

Helen squeezed Jane's hand in return.

'Yes, I know... darling,' she whispered.

Both looked around to make sure that they were alone

'Oh!' cried Jane, throwing herself into Helen's arms and sought out her lips. Moments later they were kissing each other passionately. Oh how she had longed to do this before, but had never dared to do so with all the nuns around.

The vivacious Helen now took the initiative, her hand slipping down towards Jane's breasts. Soon she was kissing her virginal pink nipples... Their hands slipped further down... Both could feel their themselves being aroused in the secret way that hitherto they had used their own fingers to achieve. Oh yes, each was thinking, her little beauty bud was her special and very secret pride and joy.

It was thrilling and very exciting to find it being touched by another girl.

But before things could move onto a more intimate plain, they suddenly heard approaching footsteps. A nun had been sent to fetch them to have their "leaving photographs" taken.

Hastily they straightened their dresses and pushed back their hair. If the nun suspected anything then she did not say a word. After all, these girls were about to go out into the wide world.

The photographs would cleverly catch their now wistful and frustrated looks. They would each give the other a precious signed copy, the sight of which would be made all the more piquant by the memory of the frustrated arousal that had preceded the photography.

Chapter 3 - The Entrapment of Miss Jane Carmichael

It was fine April morning and Jane was sewing in her small bedroom in her guardian's house.

It was only a few days after Jane had left the convent and tearfully said goodbye to Helen who would be leaving that day for Constantinople with Maria. Oh how lovely their farewell had been! Now, her education finished, Jane had come to the house of her guardian only to find herself not wanted.

When she arrived, she had proudly given her guardian the photograph that the nuns had taken of her in her first grown-up dress, thinking that he in turn would give it pride of place in his drawing room. But he had seemed unimpressed and his jealous old housekeeper, Mrs Stout, had quickly removed it.

Jane looked at the photograph of the vivacious, lovely, dark haired Helen that lay on her dressing table. At least Mrs Stout hadn't touched that. She must by now be just about arriving in Constantinople, travelling First Class in the exciting-sounding Orient Express. Lucky girl! How disappointed she had been when her guardian had refused to pay for her to go out with Helen, also to stay with Maria's parents. What a nasty old man he was!

Far from welcoming Jane into his house her guardian, a selfish elderly bachelor, had continually repeated to her his constant moan about her now being penniless. He kept saying he had had to spend on her education all the small amount of money that her parents had left - and money of his own as well. Jane was sure that the real cause of the trouble was Mrs Stout, who had previously ruled the household and who now resented the sudden arrival of a pretty young woman. Clearly she was determined to blacken Jane's name.

She glanced again at the photograph of Helen on her dressing table. Oh how she missed her! How exciting, she kept thinking, it would have been to go on the Orient Express with her friends. How sad that her guardian had put his foot down and stopped her.

Suddenly Jane was appalled to hear the sour voice of her guardian's bad - tempered housekeeper, Mrs Stout, come wafting up through the open window from the street of the small Devon town, where she was talking to one of her cronies.

'Bah! That girl may give herself all the airs and graces of a lady, but let me tell you, she's nothing but a strumpet. She's just a scheming little tart who's planning to bewitch her guardian, that fine old man. I've told him that what she needs is a good spanking. And I've told him that if he won't do it, then I will!'

Jane was incensed. How dare the old witch talk about her in this way? And a spanking! At her age! No one had ever dared to touch her. She would die of shame!

Later that morning her guardian stormed into her room where she was still quietly sewing.

'Now Miss, it's about time you understood that I'm sick and tired of paying for your keep, so that you can just sit around and do nothing.'

Jane jumped up in alarm. Clearly Mrs Stout had been getting at him again.

'But I would very much like to work, Sir,' she said in a humble voice.

'Work! With all the lady-like airs and graces that you put on? Look at your hands! They're not suitable for heavy work and just what did you learn to do at that convent that I was stupid enough to send you to? Eh?'

'Well, Sir, I know about lots of things: cooking, making clothes, embroidery... I'm sure I'll make a very good housewife.'

'Embroidery! Bah! But that's about all you'll have to offer a husband! Just remember that you'll have no dowry at all. You'll never get a husband.'

Poor Jane burst into tears. Her guardian began to walk up and down, glancing at her.

'Well I must admit she's pretty enough to have a bit of fun with,' she heard him mutter to himself. Then he turned to the girl and looked her up and down. 'I must say you're a devilish pretty girl, Jane!'

Jane was too shocked to say a word. She preferred his earlier anger to this awful attempt at flirtation.

'Stop snivelling!' cried her guardian. 'I like a girl to be fun and amusing.'

'What reason have I to be fun and amusing? Tell me that!' the girl replied.

'Oh, go to the devil then!' shouted her guardian. Then he calmed down. 'Come, my dear, give us a little smile!'

He came up behind her and put his hand on her shoulder. She looked down at her sewing, but could feel his now panting breath on her neck.

'Mrs Stout tells me you want to spend a lot on clothes,' he whispered gently.

'Nonsense!' Jane cried. 'That's just not true! I'll make do with the allowance you kindly give me. I know I'm just a wretched penniless orphan.'

'Good! I'm not criticising your desire for nice things. On the contrary, if you're nice to me, then I'm sure we can arrange to buy you some lovely things...'

Jane could not stop herself from recoiling in disgust. God, how crude! It might be the first time that a man had propositioned her, but she recognised it for what it was. She rose to her feet, pale, her heart beating hard in her breast.

'Now, now, don't make a song and dance out of it,' laughed her guardian. 'You're playing the injured innocent, but Mrs Stout tells me that you're really quite a little flirt!'

That wretched Mrs Stout, thought Jane. Everything always comes back to the awful housekeeper. Clearly her guardian believed everything that Mrs Stout told him about her, no matter how nasty it was. Perhaps if she were to be nice, to use the expression of her horrible old would-be seducer, then she might be able to get rid of the awful old woman. But to be nice to this nasty old man? She simply could not bring herself to do it. He was so awful!

Instead she turned to go, but he barred her way.

'Stay, my dear,' he said in a hoarse voice. 'Don't be angry!'

It was the first time he had spoken to her so kindly. But it only made her feel more frightened. She remembered what the sisters at the nunnery had said about not letting herself be taken in by men.

Her guardian took her hand and tried to push towards a large sofa. His eyes glittered under his grey hair and his mouth was twisted into a horrible grin. She found herself trembling.

'Don't be frightened, little thing,' he said in a strained voice. 'Just be nice to me - very nice.'

Again the same expression, Jane thought. Suddenly he thrust his lips forward and tried to kiss her. Horrified she tried to recoil, but he held her tight. Then suddenly he let her go.

'Look out, here's Mrs Stout!' he murmured like a little boy who had been caught stealing sweets.

Indeed there she was, standing in the doorway, looking sourly at the scene of the elderly man who was holding Jane in his arms.

'Oh! I see,' she said icily. 'I did not mean to interrupt you, Sir.'

'Mrs Stout!' cried Jane pushing her guardian away. 'Please don't speak like that! It's not what you think.'

'Shut your mouth, you little snake in the grass,' the older woman angrily replied. 'You're just nothing but a little man-crazy tart!'

'Don't you speak to me like that!' cried Jane. 'How dare you!'

'Ha! I'll speak to you as I like. You're not the Mistress of this house - not yet you aren't. You're nothing but a disgusting trollop. Fancy trying to seduce a poor old man who's been so kind to you. My goodness, if I was the mistress of this house, I'd soon pull up your skirts and give you a good sound thrashing, here and now!'

Jane's guardian smiled. Instead of defending her, he seemed to find his housekeeper's suggestion amusing. Encouraged by his silence, the housekeeper strode up to her, her hands raised.

'Don't touch me! Don't touch me, or I'll jump out of the window!'

'Ah, ah!' said the woman in a nasty tone of voice. 'So our cocksure little Miss is frightened of a beating, is she? Don't pretend that it'll be the first time that a man has seen your naked bottom!'

Jane was horrified by this talk. She turned back to her guardian.

'Are you going to just stand there and let me be insulted?'

'No,' the said the man angrily, terrified of having annoyed his all-powerful housekeeper. 'I've had had enough of scenes like this. You can go to the devil, Jane! Mrs Stout is quite right, there's been nothing but trouble ever since you came here... I want you out of this house as soon as possible.'

Appalled, Jane turned and left the room. Her world was falling in on her. What on earth would happen to her? Where could she go? How lucky Helen was to have a guardian who had at least agreed to pay for her to go to stay with Maria in Constantinople.

But her guardian was too frightened about what people would say, if he just threw her out. Instead he told her the following day that he was going to find her a position. He would then have done his duty and could wash his hands of her. Grateful at not being turned out, Jane thanked him.

But she was horrified when later she heard her guardian and the housekeeper constantly having rows over her. The housekeeper now really hated her.

'I want her to go,' Jane heard her shout, 'and go as far away as possible. If you won't pay her journey, then I will!'

Jane heard her guardian agree.

A week later all was settled. Jane's guardian sent for her and, in front of Mrs Stout, told her that she would be leaving for London. They had found her a good job in a dress shop which, Jane was surprised to hear, was so keen to have her that they had even agreed to pay her journey. Her guardian explained that he had replied to an advertisement for young and pretty sales girls and had sent her photograph, the one she had so proudly brought back from the convent, together with details of her age, and background. The reply, offering her a post, had just arrived, together money for the journey and the request that she go London on the evening train.

'So, Miss,' added the dreaded Mrs Stout, 'all that now remains for you to do is to thank your guardian for all that he has done for you and, if you can, to behave like a respectable girl when you get to London.'

Jane shrugged her shoulders angrily. Of course she would behave properly - she was a well brought up convent girl. All she wanted in life was the chance to work hard and marry a nice young man. Why should this bitter old woman constantly make these nasty insinuations?

Jane's meagre luggage was soon packed. It all seemed a great adventure. So much had happened since she had left the convent only two weeks before.

When she arrived in London, Jane was met at the station by a charming and smiling woman, who instantly put her at her ease. She expected to be taken straight to the shop. But instead she was she found herself in a gloomy tall building that seemed rather like a hotel.

There was no one in sight and the woman quickly took her into the building, almost before she had time to look around at the surroundings. She did not, she realised, know the name of the road or even the part of London she was in.

The woman now quickly led Jane up into a room that looked out onto a little garden beyond which was a high wall.

Jane wanted to ask the woman a mass of questions about her future but the woman cut her short, saying with a nice smile that she would be starting work in a few days' time and that meanwhile she should rest and enjoy herself. But she did not dare to let Jane go out, since Jane did not know London and all sorts of nasty things could happen to a pretty girl like her.

Jane found that indeed her room and meals had all been paid for and that all she had to do was to wait patiently until her new employers were ready for her to start work. Jane felt happy and relaxed, for the woman was all smiles and compliments.

The following morning Jane had a visitor - a male visitor. At first she wasn't quite sure whether she liked him or not. Certainly he was very polite, almost too much so - rather like the woman who was telling him in a rather exaggerated way what a pretty nice girl Jane was.

The man was clearly not English - his skin was too sallow and his eyes too black. He spoke with a foreign accent and asked Jane several innocuous questions. Had she found the journey tiring? Was she in good health? Was she sad at having to leave her family? When Jane said tearfully that she was an orphan with no relations interested in her, he seemed strangely pleased. She wondered why.

Jane was embarrassed by the way he kept looking her up and down, and smiling in a satisfied way. It all seemed rather strange. Then, when he went out with the woman, Jane was surprised to hear them talking about her in the corridor. The man was asking if she was good tempered and easy to deal with, to which the woman said something, with a laugh, about nothing that the cane could not cure.

The cane! A beating! No one, thought Jane, horrified, is going lay a hand on me! Anyway, she then said to herself reassuringly, here in London there's always the police to run to if things go wrong.

Later the woman came back into Jane's room saying that Mr Claritees, as he was called, had been delighted to meet her and had said that he would look after her. Jane drew herself up and haughtily replied that that she did not intend to get married at the tender age of eighteen, nor become any man's mistress. Whereupon the woman burst out laughing, and kissing Jane said that Mr Claritees' intentions were entirely honourable and that she could have complete confidence in him. He had the greatest respect for Jane, the woman had added with a little smile.

Now reassured, Jane thought she must have misheard when she thought the woman spoke about a caning.

But the woman's most important news was that Mr Claritees had told her that the shop in which Jane was going to work was not yet ready. Jane found this very worrying. She could not go on living alone in her room doing nothing but read and sew.

So she was delighted at first when Mr Claritees returned a couple of days later. Now perhaps she could start work. But instead he told her that he had just heard that the company who had wanted to employ her had gone bankrupt.

Poor Jane was appalled at the collapse of all her hopes, but he told her not to despair. As she was clearly a well educated and determined young woman, he could perhaps offer her a better job with some friends of his who ran a dress shop, just like the one she had planned to join. And, he added, the job was not merely a sales assistant, but Assistant Manager - with good prospects of becoming the Manager.

Jane was thrilled. Her whole face lit up. Assistant Manager! What a start in life - and perhaps, before long, Manager!

Seeing Jane's obvious elation, the Mr Claritees paused. Then he went on. 'There is just one little problem. The job is abroad!'

'Abroad! Oh, how exciting! I've always longed to travel. I do speak a little French you know. Tell me where will it be? Paris? Or Brussels?

'Not quite!' laughed Mr Claritees. 'But just as exciting for you. It's the Paris of the Levant, a very cosmopolitan town, with European shops and a large European population.'

Where?' cried Jane enthusiastically. 'It sounds wonderful.'

'Constantinople!'

'Constantinople? Goodness! That's the capital of Turkey. That was where Helen had gone to - to stay with the family of another girl at the school, Maria.'

Maria had often spoken about how beautiful and cosmopolitan it was and how a powerful Sultan ruled it. It had all sounded very exciting and she had been so very disappointed when her guardian had refused to pay for her ticket so that she could go and stay there too. And now she off there after all! How surprised and delighted her two friends would be to see her there.

'It sounds marvellous! But... I don't speak Turkish,' she stammered.

'Oh don't worry about that,' replied Mr Claritees. 'French is the second language of the educated classes in Turkey - and of all the many rich Europeans, Greeks and Armenians who live in Constantinople. They say there are more Christians in Constantinople than Moslems. So you'll have plenty of chance to practice your French.'

19

Then he laughed and went on: 'Anyway, because of your job you'll soon find yourself learning Turkish as well.'

'Well... it does all sound very interesting... But it's rather far away... I don't know...'

Then the nice woman came and kissed her, whispering into her ear to accept Mr Claritees' kind offer. She added that she felt like a mother to her and for this reason had not hesitated to pay all Jane's expenses, but that she was not rich and could not go on doing so for ever. She was so worried about what would happen to Jane if she refused this wonderful offer and had nowhere else to go.

Jane, too, found the prospect of being turned out into the street terrifying. Would she be picked up by the police and returned in shame to her guardian? She remembered how the awful Mrs Stout had threatened to beat her, like a naughty little girl. She realised that her guardian would not stop the horrible housekeeper from doing so. Indeed he would probably encourage her. My God! Anything would be better than going back to that!

Jane looked at Mr Claritees. He was so nice and respectable looking. She asked him several questions about the job in Constantinople and found that he knew a lot about it. He even showed her letters from Turkey, written in French on the letterhead of what seemed to be a large company, asking him to find them an honest, respectable and well educated English girl, who could quickly take over the running of the establishment. It did seem a wonderful opportunity - and the pay sounded out of this world.

Jane told Mr Claritees that she would have to think about it, but in fact she had already made up her mind to accept the offer. After all, London or Constantinople, what difference did it make to a poor orphan girl like her with no roots, friends or relations?

After Mr Claritees left, Jane confided all this to the nice woman and asked if she still agreed. The woman assured her that she had nothing to fear, that it was a wonderful opportunity. The respectable Mr Claritees would accompany her on the ship to make sure she was all right, but would not touch a hair of her head. And as for the business in Constantinople, had she not seen the letters? What more could she want? And, moreover, she was a grown-up woman now and could decide for herself what she wanted to do. If anything went wrong, then there was always the British Embassy there to help her.

A day later Jane and Mr Claritees left by train for Marseilles where they immediately embarked in a passenger ship sailing for the Levant, as the Near East was then called. Before leaving she had asked the nice woman to send a telegram to her guardian explaining what had happened. The woman told Jane that she had done so and, as there was no reply, she felt quite free to leave.

Once onboard, Mr Claritees could not have been more charming if she had been his daughter. He made her promise not to talk to anyone and especially not to tell anyone that she was travelling with him to Constantinople to take up a job. The Turkish police, he said, were very suspicious about foreigners working in Turkey, and might turn her back.

In fact, poor Jane was so seasick that she hardly left her cabin until the ship finally docked in Constantinople after dark. Then she was so exhausted that she scarcely noticed the colourful Eastern crowd on the darkened quayside. She noticed that the other passengers were clearly planning to stay onboard until the morning.

'Will we stay onboard, too?' she asked her travelling companion.

'No, no,' he replied. 'We'll disembark now, whilst it's still dark and the Turkish Police are asleep.'

They took a horse-drawn cab and, although it was now night, he insisted on drawing the curtains, because of the police he said. So she could see little of where they going. Off they set for the hotel at a smart trot and then climbed up what seemed to be a long hill.

Jane mused over how her arrival here was just like her arrival in London. Once again, arriving at their destination, there was no one in sight. Mr Claritees took her straight up to a comfortable room that might have been a hotel room in Europe, except that there was a strange iron grille over the window. She learned that her new employer was eager to meet her and would be coming to see her the following morning. I do hope I please her, thought Jane!

How silly she had been to hesitate about coming to Turkey. It all seemed so quiet and tranquil. Her English school friends had been convinced that civilisation ended at Dover. But, she thought, they would have been astonished to find a room like hers - and moreover in such a nice quiet hotel.

Moments later her feelings changed when she heard voices, shrill voices, talking in a language she could not understand. She recognised the voice of Mr Claritees. He seemed to be talking to a woman and she could have sworn they kept mentioning her name. Still, she thought, that's not very surprising.

They seemed to be bargaining about something and again she heard her name. Then she heard a clinking noise, as if coins were being poured out and counted. Mr Claritees now seemed to be in a very good mood, as if he had been paid for something. Jane heard him and his companion both laugh aloud. She tried to open the door a crack to see what was going on, but she found that it was locked. How very odd!

Jane heard Mr Claritees and the woman continue to talk in this strange language. She kept hearing her name mentioned and twice when the woman did so her name was marked by a strange noise which had the effect of making Mr Claritees laugh even more. What could the noise be? It sounded like the cracking of a whip.

For a moment she was terrified. Then she pulled herself together. Her guardian's dreadful old housekeeper was far away and there was no one here interested in punishing her. Anyway no one had the right to do so.

Exhausted from the journey, her head buzzing with ideas, she soon fell fast asleep.

Chapter 4 - Miss Helen Hamilton Starts Her Constantinople Diary

1st May 1900

I'm just starting this special secret diary. It's got a lock on it to stop anyone else reading it.

Life here on the banks of the beautiful Bosphorus seems so different and exciting that I felt I must write it all down. At school the nuns kept telling me that I wrote well, but I always longing to have something to write about. Well, I think I will have plenty to describe here

I arrived here yesterday with Maria Mavroyeni, my school friend back in England, on the fabulous train, the Orient Express. Her parents met the train at the station which is down by the banks of Bosphorus in the old part of the town. As well as being delighted to see their daughter again, Maria's parents could not have made me, a stranger, more welcome too.

But it was Turkey that really caught my attention - a glimpse of a new and exciting world. The place was teeming with people - the men wearing long robes or baggy trousers and shirts with simple turbans on their heads and the women veiled and wearing black shrouds. Huge mosques with towering minarets dominated the town. You could see that this is the capital of the Moslem world.

But I hardly had time to take it all in before Maria's parents had taken us in their carriage over the Galatea Bridge which runs across an inlet of the Bosphorus called the Golden Horn to Pera, the modern quarter of this huge town.

The contrast could not have been greater. We might have been in Paris with European-looking houses and shops, and strolling European men in black morning coats taking off their shiny top hats to beautiful women dressed in the latest fashions from the Rue de Rivoli. Flaunting their fashionably corseted, hourglass, figures, and low cut long flowing Fin de Siècle dresses, the young women might have been on their way to flirt with handsome young men at a Thé Dansant.

Here in Pera there were also Turkish men, described by Maria as Beys and Pashas and members of the educated Turkish class of Ottoman officials, who were similarly dressed in European-style morning coats or uniforms coats, but wearing red fezzes instead of top hats

Maria says there are more Christians than Moslems in Constantinople: a cosmopolitan mixture of Greeks, Armenians, Georgians, Bulgarians, and Lebanese from the Christian provinces of the still huge Ottoman Empire, as well large numbers of French, German and even British bankers, businessmen, engineers and diplomats - as well as German officers from the large military mission and Royal Navy officers from the British naval mission.

Maria's father is evidently rich and a leading member of the large Greek community here in Constantinople. Both he and his pretty wife are charming and very civilised. They have a big house and I have a lovely room, next to Maria's. We all speak French, which seems to be the Lingua Franca of Constantinople's cosmopolitan society. Thank Heavens the nuns taught me to speak it so well.

Tomorrow we're going to have an easy day and then in the evening, Maria says, we are off boating on the Bosphorus - to see the sophisticated life of the cosmopolitan elite of Constantinople. It all sounds very exciting and civilised.

I keep thinking of poor Jane and the interrupted secret pleasure we were about to give each other that last day of term. How she'd have loved coming out here. What more secret delicious fun we'd have had together. How cruel of her guardian not to have allowed her to accept Maria's invitation, too.

Chapter 5 - Plans for the French Slavewoman's Future

'Yes,' repeated the Sultan, 'I think we'll have a little pleasuring from this beautiful Frenchwoman - as a prelude to more intimate pleasures later on.'

Tulip salaamed and bowed. It would indeed be a great honour for a young eunuch, like himself, to supervise The Giving of Pleasure. He smiled as he remembered how this older French girl had been to be trained to do just that by him and his young friend, Agha Kasim's assistant eunuch. Under the constant threat of their canes, she had been deeply humiliated. The fact that they were both clearly younger than herself had made her humiliation all the greater.

'You keep head still!' ordered the boy in broken French.

'Yes, Sir,' answered the woman deferentially. Woe betide, she knew only too well, any woman in the harem who did show the greatest respect to a eunuch - no matter how young he might be.

Tulip slipped the bridle of her muzzle back over her head. The black leather muzzle itself was carefully shaped to fit close up under her nose, cover her mouth and fit round under her chin. This both kept her mouth covered and prevented her from pulling the muzzle up.

In the centre of the muzzle was a little flap held down with press-studs. When the flap was raised, a hole was displayed, designed so that even a reluctant girl could be made by her overseer's cane to thrust out her tongue to lick silently her Master's manhood.

Alternatively, of course, the Master's manhood could be thrust through the hole and into the woman's mouth. Two rubber projections on either side of the inside of the muzzle fitted over her teeth and prevented her from committing the sacrilege of closing her mouth - or even worse, biting the Imperial manhood. They also ensured her silence.

Tulip held her nose to make her open her mouth to take the rubber projections and then secured the muzzle under her chin. She was now very effectively muzzled. However, to prevent her from pulling the muzzle down or off, two straps were attached to the top corners. From here they ran up past her nostrils to merge, on the bridge of her nose, into one strap that went over her head. This was buckled at the back of her neck to two other straps running back from the side of the muzzle.

Similarly, to prevent the strap that went over her head being pulled down, it was attached at the crown of her head to two other straps that ran down in front of her ears to the straps running back from the sides of the muzzle her mouth to behind her neck.

Tulip tested it and adjusted some of the buckles. Yes, the harness holding it was nice and tight and her silence was assured. Only her frightened eyes disclosed her anxiety. He undid the press studs and pulled back the little flap, disclosing the tip of her tongue.

'Tongue out!' he ordered, emphasising his order with a sharp tap of his cane across the girl's thinly covered bottom. The girl had no option but to dutifully and silently thrust her tongue out through the hole.

'Stand up, girl!' came his shrill unbroken voice. Again he tapped her bottom with his dog whip. 'Show yourself to your Master!'

Nervously eyeing the boy's dog whip, Madeleine jumped up and bent down. There was a rattle of her manacles as she stepped over them. Her hands were now held behind her back - a position that pulled her bolero back from her exposed breasts. She parted her legs and slightly bent her knees to display through her transparent trousers her hairless mound and the padlocked laces that held her outer labia tightly sewn together.

Nervously she raised her head and looked straight ahead. She was a picture of well-disciplined silent womanhood with her tongue thrust out through the hole in her muzzle - ready to lick.

The Sultan smiled at the thought that later that night, she would at last be made to give up her virginity - fastened down for his pleasure, muzzled and helpless. Young Tulip would be discreetly hidden behind the curtains, ready with his dog whip to stimulate, if necessary, the woman into greater activity. The eunuchs would have told her what a great honour it was to have her virginity taken by the Shadow of Allah of on Earth. But being muzzled she would not be able to express her repugnance at what was happening and only her eyes would show her real horror.

He smiled again at the thought that at the procession to the mosque for next Friday's prayers, Agha Selim would be proudly displaying a blood spotted sheet. Once again a scarlet cross at the corner of the sheet would tell the cheering crowds that the unknown virgin had been a hated Christian.

The Sultan, pleased with this public display of his continuing virility, would then reward Agha Selim with a sum that far exceeded the cost of the woman. It would be a fine scene, though not as a fine as that when one of Selim's rivals, Agha Ali the Commander of the Orta of Balkan girls, had recently similarly displayed the virgin blood of three of his Romanian girls.

Meanwhile, the Sultan thought, the woman might as well give him a little preliminary pleasure with her tongue.

It was just at this moment that there was a discreet knock on the door. Agha Selim, the Commander of the Frenchwoman's parent Orta, who as an Agha or Master also held the rank of Bimbashi or Colonel, entered the room and salaamed respectfully. He was always eager for the Frenchwoman to earn him more money from a grateful Sultan.

The Imperial Harem was organised on military lines with the junior eunuchs having the rank of officers, the Aghas that of Colonel and the all important Kizlar Aghasi, the Sultan's chief black eunuch, that of a general - whilst the women were the well-disciplined rank and file.

The Agha nodded to Tulip, his subordinate officer, who was still holding in one hand the woman's lead and in his other his raised bamboo cane. Yes, he thought, the boy was coming on well. One day he, too, might be an Agha in charge of one of Ortas into which the women in the harem were divided.

Agha Selim was accompanied by his fellow Agha, Manju, the dreaded Agha of the Curved Bellies - dreaded because he was always promenading around the harem, sizing up the half naked women. He always on the look-out for any whom he would felt particularly please the Sultan with a well curved belly and whom he would recommend to the Kizlar Aghasi to be handed over to him.

Manju was one of the most experienced eunuchs in the Imperial Harem and was a trained midwife. He was an expert at picking out a succession of Christian girls, of different ages and heights, as being suitable for a forced maternity - to be crossed with one or more of the Sultan's giant African Dinka Black Guards. Once mated, he kept them slim - the better to show off their beautifully swelling bellies.

It was his responsibility to parade before the Sultan a dozen beautiful, and interestingly different, naked curved bellies. These would range from bellies which were only "just showing", to use the eunuchs' cruel expression, to one at least that was hugely and excitingly curved - thanks to Agha Manju's skill in delaying deliveries. This was something which might have been dangerous, were it not for the invariable small size heads of the half Dinka progeny.

Moreover, the nervous women in the harem could not count on the Aghas of their own Ortas to resist the demands for forced breeding of the Agha of the Curved Bellies - for there was fierce competition between the rival Aghas for one of their girls to be the next to be chosen for an enforced motherhood. There might be no financial reward for a girl who successfully excited the interest of the Sultan, by having her increasingly swelling naked belly regularly displayed before him. But for the Agha of her Orta there most certainly would be.

It was scarcely surprising, therefore, that the Agha of Curved Bellies was regarded by all the women in the harem with extra fear and trepidation - for they could never be sure when his approving glance might suddenly fall upon them. Once a girl was selected for motherhood, the Agha of her Orta would hand her over temporarily to his colleague the Agha of the Curved Bellies. He would be in charge of her mating and of her subsequent progress until she had dutifully produced her little new mulatto slave, who would be immediately taken away, to be brought up to labour on one of the Sultan's estates.

During the selected girl's maternity her own Agha would, in conjunction with Agha of the Curved Bellies, satisfy himself with the state of her increasingly curved belly, making sure that it was constantly shown off to the delighted Sultan.

Both Aghas were wearing red fezzes and were incongruously dressed in identical Stamboulines, the black morning coats worn by all senior officials of the Ottoman Empire. In the right hand buttonholes of the Stamboulines of both Aghas glistened an embossed silver Imperial crest, showing that they had the rank of Agha in the personal service of the Sultan with the right to administer up to twenty five strokes of the cane or whip to any woman in their charge.

In Selim's left buttonhole, like that of Tulip's, also gleamed the green enamel crest of the Syrian Orta which he commanded. Manju wore the crest of the Orta of Curved Bellies - a new moon, shaped like the belly of a well pregnant slavegirl. His was a much smaller command but one that was highly regarded because of its close relationship with the Sultan himself.

Whereas Selim was proudly carrying the normal silver tipped cane of an Agha, Manju was holding the coiled-up thong of a short well-oiled whip. The use of the cane on one of his pregnant slave girls, he was always explaining, was not to be recommended. But a well directed whip was quite harmless.

'Once Your Highness has taken this woman's virginity,' Selim now murmured, 'she will no longer, of course, be eligible to continue as one Your Highness's Gedekli. We were therefore wondering what you had in mind for her?'

'Yes, we were both thinking, Your Highness,' added the Agha of the Curved Bellies, in a persuasive tone of voice, 'that it would a shame to deprive such a delightful creature of the joys of conception - wanted or not.'

The Sultan's eyes gleamed at the thought of this lovely Frenchwoman being made to perform in the tiled mating pit or kept in a cage for the Black Guards to use as they came off duty, whilst he was dealing with those infuriating French bankers. He imagined how, whilst they were arguing, the Kizlar Aghasi would silently slip into the room and whisper the welcome news that the beautiful Frenchwoman was ready to receive up inside her the fertilising semen of a black giant - just when the experienced Agha of Curved Bellies had said she was ready to conceive.

Later on Agha Manju had her ready, bitted and bridled like a favourite brood mare, to be paraded before him with her curved belly showing well. In both cases he would adjourn the meeting for a short interval whilst he dealt with an urgent "domestic matter" - and to return with his self-confidence boosted.

'Nor, Your Highness,' said the Agha of the Curved Bellies, 'should we wish to deprive you of the unique pleasure of watching a Frenchwoman going through a first enforced maternity.'

'Yes,' whispered Agha Selim. 'Think, Your Highness, of the pleasure it would give you to have the growing belly of this Frenchwoman, reluctant mother-to-be, being displayed before you - quite apart from when you were having a difficult meeting with those French bankers.'

He gestured with both hands as if holding a well curved belly. 'Imagine,' he went on, 'watching her increasing dismay as she sees her now flat little belly gradually swelling with its growing black progeny.'

'And, of course,' added the Agha of Curved Bellies with a cruel laugh, 'watching her desperation as she realised that she was unable to prevent Nature taking its full course - thanks to being carefully locked up in a chain mail breeding belt.'

'Yes, Your Highness,' continued Agha Selim cunningly, 'it would indeed be a very suitable revenge for all the slights and humiliations the infidel French bankers have heaped upon your Highness and our great empire.'

The Sultan nodded eagerly. Their remarks coincided with his thoughts.

These same remarks were, however, accompanied by gasps of horror from under Madeleine's muzzle, for having spent so long in the Orient she understood enough Turkish to realise what was being said to the Sultan. Moreover it so degrading having to listen in silence, like an animal, as the awful men discussed their future breeding plans for her.

The Frenchwoman blushed and made further little protesting noises from under her muzzle as Agha Selim now reached forward and slowly lowered the woman's silken pantaloons. Then, as Agha Selim held the blushing woman quite still, the Agha of Curved Bellies ran his hand expertly over her hips and down over her bare belly.

'With these excellent child bearing hips,' he said, 'she should have no difficulty in carrying and delivering for her Master a large mulatto slave, sired by one of Your Imperial Highness's larger Black Guards.'

He ran his hand over the tightly sewn up beauty lips of a Gedekli

'And she should have no trouble dropping even a large progeny from the birthing chair,' the Agha of Curved Bellies added. He was a great believer in the use of the traditional Turkish harem birthing chair, with a straw lined basket, placed under the cut-away in the seat on which was the girl was seated, ready to receive her progeny. She herself would be seated on it with her ankles strapped wide apart to the legs of the chair and her wrists raised up above her head by a pulley, so that she could be made to rise up and down to assist the delivery process.

He was also a great believer in the power of the whip at such moments. A few well-timed strokes of his whip across the Frenchwoman's belly would certainly get things going. The Frenchwoman would of course be muzzled so that her cries did not disturb the harem - or the Sultan. Furthermore, a hood would be placed over her head just as she dropped her mulatto progeny into the waiting basket so that she never saw it - never mind held it, thanks to her hands being chained above her head. It would, however, be briefly held to her breast by the Agha of the Curved Bellies to suckle the protecting initial feed, before being taken away and given to a Negress to feed and rear.

Meanwhile a tiny figure had also slipped into the room: Shu-shu, the Sultan's pet white dwarf eunuch. Whilst acting as the harmless plaything of the bored harem women, he was in reality the Sultan's secret spy. He would report on whatever rumours were sweeping the harem and whether one or more of the women, perhaps even one of the Kadins, was getting too big for her boots and needed a thrashing to bring her to heel.

He would also secretly give the Sultan his views on which of the girls would please him best in bed, especially if, whether she liked it or not, she was teamed up with one or more other girls.

He, too, had a vested interest in suitable girls being selected for forced breeding. For traditionally the dwarf was also in charge of the Sultan's elite team of white milkmaids, one of whose milk-laden breasts were offered to the Sultan first thing every morning and one of whom knelt discreetly out sight in the Sultan's sumptuous bedroom, at night and during his siesta, ready to offer him a refreshing stimulant after he had enjoyed his chosen women.

'And then...' whispered the dwarf, reaching up to pull apart Madeleine's open bolero to reveal two delightfully full and mature breasts, tipped with still virginal nipples. He began expertly to feel the firm breasts. 'These would milk well, Your Highness. She would make a fine addition to your team of milkmaids: a Frenchwoman's milk!'

The Sultan also reached out and felt a warm breast. Again he nodded in agreement.

Agha Selim smiled. He would make certain that the dwarf concentrated on maintaining a good flow of milk so that, when sent for, the girl's breasts were overflowing and ready by day or night to revive her Master and quench his thirst.

'Of course,' added the dwarf, 'we would have to stretch her nipples with tight silken threads so that she could properly offer her milk to the Padishah.'

Agha Selim nodded. He would certainly be making sure, in conjunction with the little white dwarf, that whilst her belly was swelling her nipples were being gradually extended until they were judged to be sufficiently long for the Sultan to suck easily - or to have her milked for his consumption.

Of course, just as a heifer is "steamed up" before calving by being given high protein food to ensure a proper flow of milk, so her Agha would be checking that she was given special food. Furthermore, as the sire of her child was a giant Dinka, Nature would further ensure that her breasts would swell up to produce sufficient milk to feed her large infant - milk that, of course, would now be available to meet the requirements of his Imperial Highness.

'Or, perhaps if one of the Kadins bears your own Imperial child, then we could use this woman as a wet nurse?' added Agha Selim.

'An interesting thought,' murmured the Sultan. He had indeed been wondering whether it was time he fathered another son.

Then, putting aside these plans for the future, the Sultan waved away the dwarf and the two older eunuchs, who left the room bowing and smiling. They were satisfied that they had aroused the Sultan's keen interest in their plan for the French slavegirl's future. He would discuss the matter with his chief confidant when it came to his women - the Kizlar Aghasi, whom doubtless the other eunuchs would have already briefed.

The Sultan rang a bell and two pretty young blond Circassian girls ran into the room, their half-exposed breast bouncing arousingly. The girls were the Frenchwoman's companions: virgins from the Sultan's dozen specially trained Gedekli, or maids-in-waiting. They were followed by Kasim, the newly promoted, youthful eunuch Agha of the Gedekli. As always he was carrying the long thin silver tipped bamboo cane with which he enforced strict discipline amongst the young virgins and the older Frenchwoman in his charge.

He exchanged a nod with his colleague, Tulip.

'Prepare your Master!' he ordered.

The two girls obediently knelt in front of the Sultan and deftly parted his robes. Whilst one girl ran her hands up under the Sultan's robe and squeezed his nipples, the other gently took his manhood in her hands and brought him to erection.

Meanwhile, Tulip had unfastened the little flap in the front of the Madeleine's muzzle.

The Sultan then waved the two pretty young Gedekli away and turned to Tulip.

'Set her to work!' he ordered.

'Crawl to Master!' the boy ordered in his piping treble, holding the Frenchwoman's lead and giving her a warning tap on her bottom with his long cane. Awkwardly, with her hands still chained behind her back and her eyes flashing in horror over her muzzle, Madeleine hesitantly edged forward on her knees between her Master's knees.

Tulip gave her another tap with his dog whip and she lowered her muzzle over the Imperial manhood, her hanging breasts making a pretty sight. With an eager grunt the Sultan thrust his manhood through the little hole into her mouth. Tulip gave her another tap with his whip. Her head began to rise and fall as she alternatively sucked and licked in the way she had been made to practice.

The Sultan snapped his fingers and pointed down.

'Cup Master with hands,' ordered the young Agha of the Gedekli.

Obediently Madeleine half rose and stepped over her manacles. Then with her hands once again in front of her, she now cupped her Master's testicles in her hands whilst again sucking his manhood.

Suddenly the Sultan raised a finger warningly. The Agha Kasim knew it was the sign that the Sultan's pleasure must be more drawn out.

'Stop!' he ordered. 'Raise head! Keep still!'

Like a well-trained circus animal, the Frenchwoman raised her head, keeping her eyes respectfully lowered. There was a long pause, then the Sultan again nodded to the young Agha.

'Tongue only!' ordered the Agha Kasim.

Tulip gave her a warning on her bottom with his cane. It was enough to make the scared Frenchwoman again strain to thrust the tip of her tongue entrancingly through the little gap in her muzzle. This was something she had often been made to practice by young Kasim, his cane tapping her scarcely covered bottom with an increasing sharpness at the slightest sign of hesitation. She now applied her tongue to the tip of her Master's manhood. Her role, she knew, was simply to spin out the giving of pleasure.

Minutes later the Sultan waved the Frenchwoman away. He did not want to spoil his ability to take her virginity that night. The two Gedekli again appeared and refastened his robe. The Sultan stood up.

'Well done!' he said to the smiling Kasim and Tulip.

The large figure of Agha Selim now re-entered the room and again bowed obsequiously to the Sultan. Meanwhile Kasim had taken Madeleine's lead from Tulip with a tap of his long cane on her bottom, and gestured to her to crawl out of the room. The Sultan looked down approvingly as the half-naked woman crawled away on all fours.

'Having an educated Frenchwoman in my power is certainly very satisfying,' he said. 'You did well to find her, Agha Selim.'

Selim bowed low, anticipating an eventual gift of a purse of gold coins.

Chapter 6 - Helen Learns About Those Terrible Turks

2nd May

What a wonderful and yet strangely frightening evening it has been. What an amazingly beautiful place Constantinople is. But, as I began to learn this evening, what an astonishingly different world the Moslem one is. I just must write it all down before going to bed.

It was a lovely warm evening and Maria was wearing a pretty flounced party dress from Paris. Seen out here she looks a typical, very pretty, Greek girl. Petite, quiet spoken and a little plump, with what I now realise is a typical olive Mediterranean complexion. Her dark hair and eyes match my own and we must have made a pretty pair.

With my small laced waist, I was dressed more for an evening on the Thames back at Henley: long skirt, little black lace-up boots, a gaily beribboned straw boater - and a tight, high necked broad-shouldered, "leg of mutton" white blouse that showed off my small firm breasts.

We were driven down to the water's edge and embarked in a long, slender, Turkish rowing boat or kayik, with an elaborately carved open-sided covering over the sternsheets to protect us from the sun or rain. It was manned by several rowers dressed in the distinctive thin white shirts, red waistcoats and red fez headdress of the Bosphorus boatmen, who took us across to the far bank of the slowly moving Bosphorus itself.

It's a sparkling strip of winding water that is surrounded by beautiful green hills, covered with tall Cypress trees - about a mile wide and about twenty miles long. Not only does it divide Europe from Asia but it also links the Black Sea to the Mediterranean.

We had joined a large number of similar kayiks that had gathered to hear a concert being given by the elderly and now deposed Khedive Ismail of Egypt from his luxurious yali or villa, on the water's edge at Emirgan a few miles up the Bosphorus from the port area of the Golden Horn.

I felt quite overcome by the beauty and romance of it all: the music, the singing, the lights of the boats, the flirtatious young men and women, unashamedly holding hands across from one boat to another or exchanging glances and flowers.

A lovely soprano voice rose up from the pretty little white pavilion on the water's edge and echoed out over the still blue Bosphorus and the gentle rolling wooded hills that bordered it.

The gorgeous voice also rolled over the mass of kayiks, moored close together to form a shifting mass of boats, like a huge raft.

I could not help noticing the admiring glances of a very handsome young Englishman, seated with a jolly party of bright young things in an adjoining kayik. To my delight, he leaned across and introduced himself. I learned that his name was David Lyons and that he was a British naval officer, apparently part of the Naval Mission in Constantinople, helping to train the Ottoman Navy.

The lovely soprano voice struck up another Aria.

'Oh what a lovely voice she has,' I said enthusiastically.

I was so astonished by what Maria then said, and said later, that I can still remember them as if she was dictating them to me as I write.

'Yes,' she said, 'they say that the Khedive prides himself on only buying women slaves with the best voices.'

'What do you mean... only buys slave women with good voices?' I asked, repeating her words incredulously. Life here in Constantinople, the meeting place of East and West, was obviously different, but even so!

I looked at the elegant young woman standing up in the pavilion, dressed in a low cut French ball gown, gesturing piteously as she sang in Italian of a lost love. Behind her stood, motionless, two little black boys dressed in satin waistcoats and bulky Turkish breeches, each wearing a white silk turban with a high ostrich feather. Little black leather whips were prominently stuck into the white sashes round their waists.

'You don't really mean that that young woman, that very European-looking woman now singing, is a slave?' I exclaimed.

Maria laughed. 'Oh yes! They say the Khedive paid a huge sum to have her secretly abducted from a European Opera House and brought here to delight him.'

When I protested that this was terrible and asked why her Ambassador had not insisted on her immediate release, Maria just laughed, saying that he probably didn't know about her - anyway not for certain, for Moslems do not discuss their women. Moreover the Ambassador was probably very happy not to know, for here in Constantinople it was best not to ask too many questions.

When I said that was terrible, Maria looked serious and explained that her family had survived here for generations by not offending the all-powerful Moslem Turks. No Christian subject of the Sultan would ever dream of asking about what goes on in the harem of a Moslem - never mind enquiring about one of his slavegirls. Furthermore no Moslem True Believer would ever dream of discussing of his women with any other man - except, of course, with his chief black eunuch, his chief confidant when it came to women.

'You mean,' I asked still very surprised, 'that the Ambassador would simply have come up against a brick wall?'

'Yes, and would have caused considerable offence into the bargain - and jeopardised his country's chances of winning some lucrative contracts in the Ottoman Empire as well.'

Then I when I asked her how she knew about such things, she said that her father is a leading businessman here - and his father and grandfather before him. 'I was brought up to know all about the Turks,' she lowered her voice, 'the terrible Turks, as we call them when no one's listening.'

'Well terrible or not,' I said, 'I can't see the British Ambassador sitting back and doing nothing if she had had been an English girl.'

'Oh, I shouldn't be too sure!' laughed Maria. She said that her father used to say that England doesn't want to rock the boat here in the Ottoman Empire - not with all those restless Moslems in India who regard the Sultan as their Caliph, their spiritual leader. He says that therefore, although the British are always pressing the Sultan to reform, it's their long standing policy to keep in with the Sultan so as to keep the Russians out - and in future perhaps the Germans too.

'But, meanwhile, how awful for that poor girl - being enslaved and having to sing in front of us.'

'Yes,' agreed Maria, 'and especially as she's having to sing the aria from Mozart's *Abduction from the Seraglio*.'

Maria went to explain that the aria was the one in which the heroine sings of her now lost love - the man she loved before she was captured and enslaved.

Good Heavens, I wondered, did this girl in real life have a lover before she was abducted? Is the poor thing really singing about her own lost love?'

'Probably,' Maria said. 'You can see she's a very beautiful young woman. Who knows, perhaps she had a husband or a lover - or both!'

'How dreadful! Poor thing! But can nothing really be done about her. Surely your family...?'

Maria shook her head. Her family had learned that it was best to ignore such things - unless they wanted their business to be ruined.

She pointed to two little black boys standing unobtrusively behind the young woman. 'They'll be her eunuch guardians.'

'Oh!' I cried, deeply shocked. I remembered secretly looking up "eunuch" in the encyclopaedia with Jane in the convent and learning that they had been gelded as a boy, just like the gelding horses that I rode at home. Poor things!

'They're probably each holding a little chain fastened to each of her ankles - just in case she should try and run away and join us. And,' went on Maria, 'by having the two boys there, the Khedive is proudly, but discreetly, showing off that this lovely woman is his slave.'

'Oh!' I again cried, 'but surely...'

My words were interrupted by a sudden change in the music. The light in the pavilion went out and instead a long barred cage was lit up. By it stood a large black man, dressed almost incongruously in a black double-breasted morning coat, the Stambouline, that is the standard Ottoman dress for officials - and apparently for eunuchs too.

The voices of a large female chorus came from behind the lattice screen of the cage. They were singing a well-known chorus from *Aida*. Maria whispered that the Khedive had commissioned Verdi to write *Aida* to celebrate the opening of the Suez Canal. Now here in retirement he boasts that he owns a chorus of a dozen white Christian slavegirls, specially trained to sing it.

'Christian girls?' I again exclaimed. 'Slaves?'

'Oh, yes,' replied Maria. She explained that most of the slavegirls here are Christian for it's against the tenets of the Moslem faith to enslave fellow Moslems. And, when I asked where on earth all the slavegirls come from, she said that thanks to the regular revolts of the Sultan's Christian subjects the supply of white slavegirls is unlikely ever to dry up.

Apparently the normal Ottoman punishment for revolting against the Sultan is the enslavement of the young wives and daughters of the hot blooded young men concerned. The slave dealers send their agents, their carts fitted with covered cages for transporting slaves, to follow the army whenever they are sent to put down a revolt. And the cages rarely come back empty.

I just could not believe my ears, but Maria said I'd be surprised at what goes on under the surface here in Constantinople. The slave market may officially be closed now, but apparently the slave dealers are as busy as ever, supplying the harems of the rich Beys and Pashas with white women. Maria reminded me of the scandal when not all that long ago it came out that Samuel Baker, famous for finding the source of the Nile, had bought the future Lady Baker as a half naked Hungarian slavegirl.

She went on to say that the apparently civilised Beys and Pashas and other senior Ottoman officials encourage their eunuchs to keep in touch with the slave dealers to check what merchandise is currently on offer. Knowing his discerning Master's likes and dislikes, and the length of his purse, a eunuch was in a good position to haggle with a dealer over a young white woman whom he felt would adorn the harem of which he was in charge.

Goodness, how shocking!

Maria paused and then laughed. 'Father says that the Beys and Pashas are getting richer and richer - and he should know for he's the banker of many of them!'

'But what's that got to do with it?' I asked.

'Simply that Turkish nature being what it is, the demand for pretty young white slavegirls in Constantinople is greater than ever.'

'What! 'I cried, adding that it must be awful to be a white slave in a rich man's harem.

Maria laughed. 'Oh they say that, were it not for the cruel eunuchs, the girls would rather enjoy life in a harem, once they've got used to it - no financial worries and all decisions being taken for you.'

'Oh! You're just exaggerating it all just to shock me,' I protested. Then pointing at the strange looking black man standing by the side of the cage, I asked what he was doing there.

I gasped when Maria replied that he would be one of the Khedive's black eunuchs in charge of his women - and was there to make sure the women all behave properly as dutiful slavegirls.

'My God!' I almost shouted, rising from my seat in the kayik.

'Shush!' whispered Maria urgently. 'The Sultan has spies everywhere.'

She went to say that they say one half of the population here is spying on the other half. Sons denounce their fathers to the Sultan and in every large household either the cook or one of the other servants is spying for the Sultan. So you have to be very careful what you say! Apparently the Sultan suspended the constitution years ago and now rules as an absolute monarch.

I couldn't, she continued, single-handedly suddenly abolish white female slavery in the Ottoman Empire. It was far too well engrained.

Not even the Sultan and his Beys and Pashas could do that - not that they would want to, for they would then lose most of the women in their harems. So, she insisted that I just sit and relax and enjoy the music and the beauty of the Bosphorus - and the attentions of the young British naval officer whose eye I seemed to have caught.

'You won't hear or see anything like this,' she said, 'when you go back to England and perhaps not here for much longer. They say that the Sultan's going to ban these concerts because he's nervous of such large gatherings and is jealous of the Khedive's popularity.'

3rd May
Early morning. Last night I tossed and turned in my comfortable bed in the Mavroyenis' big house. I was thinking back at the strangely romantic evening, about David Lyons and about all the shocking things that Maria had told her about the Khedive's slaves. It can't have been true, I decided, she must have been making it up!

How terrible and shocking it must be to be a slavegirl, the slave of a Moslem, in these modern times. Secretly I have always been fascinated by stories of the East, about harems and concubines and had avidly read anything I could find out about them. And now here they are. If it is true, slavegirls and black eunuchs really do exist!

Under the bedclothes I could feel myself becoming shamefully moist at the idea of being a slave - kept for the pleasure of one old man. How terrifying!

But I had thought with a smile, as I fell asleep, at least no English girl could really end up in a harem. Not now, not here, not in this highly civilised place, not with David Lyons to protect her - even though there still was a Sultan who reigned as an absolute ruler, apparently kept a huge harem of slave women, and who called himself the Commander of the Faithful, the Lord of the Seven Seas and the Shadow of God on Earth.

Chapter 7 - Jane in the Hands of Slave Dealers

The day after her arrival, Jane was left to sleep and rest after her journey. A hidden hand pushed her meals through a hatch in the door - and that was her only contact with the outside world.

Then that evening, just as a now much refreshed Jane was finishing dressing and had started to do her hair, she heard the door being unlocked. A large fat, sour-faced woman entered the room. She was dressed in European clothes, but she was very different from the kind woman in London. She looked like a witch and reminded Jane of the horrible Mrs Stout.

A little put out, Jane turned and wished the woman good morning. But she just muttered something in reply. Intimidated, Jane continued to dress in silence, whilst the woman watched her from under her heavy eyelids. Suddenly she broke into guttural but fluent French.

'So you're the little English girl called Jane?'

'Yes, indeed,' replied Jane.

'And you really are English?'

'Of course, born and brought up in England with English parents who are now, alas, dead,' replied Jane eagerly, delighted at the chance of trying out her own French.

'Good. Now tell me, girl, are you still a virgin?'

Jane was struck dumb with surprise, her hand still raised to arrange her hair. What a question! She must have misunderstood the woman's difficult accent. The woman gave a hideous grin. Then she again raised her harsh voice.

'Yes, Jane, I asked you if you still a virgin. It's simply question: yes or no?'

Jane blushed. Was it normal here to ask women such questions, or was it just that the woman not being very fluent in French had really meant to ask if she was virtuous? She decided that this latter must have been what the woman meant and replied that her conduct had always been exemplary.

'Hum!' said the woman, 'you certainly took your time before replying. Listen! You just be careful not to mislead me!'

'But it's true, I assure you,' cried Jane. 'No man has even kissed me.'

'Good! That's just as well then,' the older woman replied. 'But I warn you, I'm Fazileh-hanum and if you're lying to me, then you'll get a real hiding.'

'What!' Jane cried.

'Just you remember that Fazileh-hanum is very used to dealing with young women like you - and, if they lie to me, then they get the

40

whip. It's as simple as that. And no doubt, as a well brought up English girl, you've never yet been properly beaten. Well, have you?'

Jane felt herself going pale and could not find the words with which to reply. Mrs Stout had threatened her with being beaten and would, if she had had the chance, have carried out her threat. But this woman was far more frightening.

'Well, so you're scared now are you, girl? Perhaps you've already misbehaved with men, like many European girls do. But you'd better tell me if you did. You won't fool anyone here and if you're playing at being a false virgin, then you'll get a real thrashing. And it looks as though you've got a nice soft little bottom, so you'll really feel it.'

Jane's rising anger gave her back the use of her tongue even though her now dry lips made her voice halting and nervous.

'I'm not a child now,' she began, 'and I will not permit you...'

The woman interrupted her with a loud laugh.

'Oh, so the little darling won't permit me, won't she?' the woman jeered. 'Well we'll soon see, won't we? The whip always has a great effect on girls who try and resist.'

'How dare you talk to me like this,' shouted Jane in her slightly halting French. 'And anyway you've no power over me... And I'm not such a fool as you seem to think I am. And if you go on with this... this joke in bad taste... then just remember that I'm English and that I know very well that in Constantinople there's a British Embassy which will protect me. So you just be careful what you say to me! So...'

The older woman was looking Jane with her piercing eyes. She let her carry on with her protests until she ran out of breath, more frightened by the woman's silence than if she had lost her temper.

'I've heard about you young Englishwomen,' she said coldly to Jane, 'All pride and obstinacy - but still scared stiff of the whip. I know all about Christian sluts like you! I've dealt with so many of them!'

'But who are you?' cried Jane. 'What do you want with me? And just where am I, for Heaven's sake?'

The horrible older woman seemed very amused by her questions. She took her time before replying and then emphasised each word in her awful accent.

'Where are you, little girl?' She laughed. 'In the closely guarded establishment of a modern slave dealer - that's where!'

What?' cried Jane

'Yes, a slave dealer! Why do you think you've been brought here?'

'To be the well paid manageress of a dress shop, of course,' replied Jane innocently.

'And you believed that! Oh no, my girl, the only person who's going to be well paid is me - by the eunuch of a rich Bey or Pasha who decides to buy you for the harem of his Master - or, perhaps if I'm lucky, by Agha Ali for the Imperial Harem itself.'

'What!' again cried Jane, not quite understanding this talk of eunuchs and of the Imperial Harem.

'Yes, my girl, you're going to be a slavegirl in the harem of a rich and probably elderly Turk - or perhaps even have the honour of being in the seraglio of the Commander of the Faithful, the Representative of Allah, himself.'

Jane still did not fully understand what the woman was saying but the words slavegirl, harem and seraglio summed up everything awful that she had heard about the East.

'Oh my God!' she sobbed. Had she been tricked by the apparently kind woman in London and by Mr Claritees? She remembered being warned by the nuns about the White Slave Trade. She had taken that with a pinch of salt - but now apparently she was the victim of that trade herself.

She felt that she was about to burst into tears.

'But first, you must be prepared - made fit to enter the harem of a discerning rich Turkish gentleman - for they find extra pleasure in owning a virgin white girl whose own ability to enjoy certain pleasures has been dramatically curtailed - as has her ability to masturbate secretly behind his back.'

Masturbate! That was something that the girls at the convent would only whisper about when the nuns weren't listening. How shameful to hear this dreadful woman talking about it openly. But what did she mean about curtailing a girl's ability to do it. How?

'And,' she added rubbing her hands, 'they will authorise their eunuchs to pay extra for one who can't.'

Jane did not in her innocence understand what this awful woman was driving at. But the mere thought of being sold into a Turkish harem was enough to set her off.

'Never!' she screamed. 'Never! Do you hear me, you revolting creature? I'll never go into some awful harem. I'm a free Englishwoman, do you hear? You've no right to...'

The woman did not say a word in reply. Jane went on and on, becoming more and more angry. The woman continued to listen in silence and then shook her head.

'The sight of what the whip can do will soon calm you down,' she laughed cruelly.

With that she left the room, locking the door behind her.

Chapter 8 - 'Find Me an English Girl!'

The Sultan, dressed in his usual elaborate military uniform, was in a furious mood as he stepped through the small locked door, continually guarded day and night by eunuchs, which linked the huge harem wing to the rest of the Dolmabahcheh Palace to which he had moved with his harem from the Yildiz Palace up the hill. Through the adjoining tall French windows could be seen the blue sparkling waters of the Bosphorus - only a stone's throw away.

'Once again! The nerve of that fool of an Ambassador!' he exclaimed.

He had just had a meeting with the British Ambassador regarding a much-needed large loan that a group of British banks were hesitating about making to the Ottoman Empire. As usual the Ambassador had droned on about the Sultan's profligacy and had urged the Sultan to cut back on unnecessary expenditure. But this time he had even had the effrontery to mention the Imperial Harem as a possible candidate for retrenchment. The nerve of the man! The very idea!

The Ambassador had even queried whether the Sultan really needed quite so many women. This had greatly enraged the Sultan, for Moslems do not discuss their harems with other men - and certainly not with infidels. It was an insufferable insult.

Moreover, the Sultan told himself, that stupid Ambassador did not seem to realise that that Turks, the mainstay of the Ottoman Empire, expected their Sultan to maintain a large harem of mainly subjected Christian women. They were proud of it - and, hence, of him. It was an essential symbol of the continuing ascendancy of the Moslem crescent over the hated Christian cross - just as was keeping the Kurds loyal by discreetly allowing them periodically a free hand to go and massacre their disloyal Christian Armenian neighbours - and to abduct and violate their women.

Waiting for the Sultan and salaaming respectfully were two large black figures. The first one was the repulsively bloated Kizlar Aghasi, literally the "Master of the Girls", the Sultan's Chief Black Eunuch. Despite his simple African background and lack of education he was a man of considerable power and influence, for he was the Sultan's close confidant and uniquely had the title of "Highness". In the entire Ottoman Empire, he and the Grand Mufti, the religious head, ranked together second only to the Grand Vizier for whom he acted as the official go-between to the Sultan. And, of course, he was the only the man to have access to the Sultan when he was "busy" in the Imperial Harem.

Ever since the death some years earlier of the Sultan's mother, the Kizlar Aghasi had been left as the undisputed ruler of the harem. It was his proud boast no girl went to the Sultan's bed without having first been intimately inspected and approved of by him.

The second large man, a rather slimmer version of the hugely fat Kizlar Aghasi, was Agha Ali, one of the Kizlar Aghasi's principal subordinate black eunuchs. He was the Commander of the Blue Orta, also known as the Balkan Orta. It was his boast that his Orta included some of the most beautiful and desirable of the many concubines in the Imperial Harem - something that made him hated by many of his rival Aghas. It was Agha Ali's Orta that was on duty that day, during which time Ali was responsible for providing the Sultan with women for his pleasure and entertainment.

Like the Kizlar Aghasi, Agha Ali carried as a symbol of his authority a slim whippy cane-like bamboo wand with a curved handle and, in his right hand buttonhole, wore a small but distinctive Imperial crest. Whereas the wand of the Kizlar Aghasi was bound and tipped with gold and the crest in his buttonhole was of similarly of gold, the cane of Agha Ali, like those his rival Aghas, was bound and tipped with silver and the crest in his buttonhole was also of silver.

To the outside world these wands and little Imperial crests might have seemed to be merely symbolic, but not to the women of in the harem. They regarded them with dread and fear, for they all knew only too well that the gold crests conferred on the Kizlar Aghasi the right, at the slightest sign of lack of respect or for the slightest misdemeanour, to apply slowly and deliberately an unlimited number of strokes of his dreaded cane to their naked backsides - or perhaps, even worse, to the soles of their feet - a punishment that was know as the bastinado.

Similarly the silver crests authorised Agha Ali, like the other Aghas, to apply an excruciating twenty five strokes of his cane to any member of his Orta - or to report a woman of another Orta to her own Agha for punishment. Of course, any woman judged to be deserving of more than twenty five strokes would be reported to the Kizlar Aghasi himself.

The Sultan's anger slightly abated at the sight of his fawning senior eunuchs, for he knew that Agha Ali would already have arranged, with the agreement of the Kizlar Aghasi, to provide a girl or a trained team of girls to pleasure him and to temporarily ease his anger. But he also needed something more long-term.

'Bah!' he muttered to the attentively listening eunuchs, the only people to whom he could unburden himself. 'I want my secret revenge on that arrogant infidel pig of a British Ambassador.'

He paused for thought, remembering that each Agha was responsible for acquiring fresh recruits for his Orta and that each had his own budget especially for that purpose. As he thought, his face reddened with anger.

'Oh, yes' he burst out. 'I'd pay anything to the first Commander of an Orta in my harem who can produce a pretty English virgin for me to slake my revenge on.'

He stroked his chin.

'Yes' he went on, 'I'll reward the first eunuch who can produce a well educated and pretty young Englishwoman for me. I want to see her kept in the Court of Innocent Virgins, awaiting my pleasure and the loss of her virginity. Then the next time I have to listen to that pompous ass, the British Ambassador, giving me another sermon on raising the status of women in the Ottoman Empire, I shall be thinking of her - and deciding whether it is now time to take her.'

He laughed.

'Just think! It would more than make up for having to listen to that insolent dog preaching me about my iniquities and that of us so called "useless" Turks if unknown to him one of his precious young Englishwomen was waiting, tied down in my harem, for me to take her virginity - just as I took that of the Frenchwoman of Agha Selim's when the French bankers were so annoying me.'

'Or, perhaps,' then whispered the cunning Kizlar Aghasi who know just what to say to arouse his Master, 'bent over naked and trembling in front of you - ready for her Agha's cane on her bottom, with ten strokes coming to her for each of the infidel Ambassador's insults... Think of the pleasure of hearing her screaming for mercy - and, in her pain, being made to denounce both the Ambassador and Great Britain itself.'

'Yes, that's what I'd like to hear! An English Miss, a Christian dog, screaming for mercy as she felt the cane across her bare bottom! Owned by me, the Ottoman Sultan, the man the English say they so despise! Yes, I'd love that.'

'And,' added the Kizlar Aghasi, 'the beauty would be that the infidel pig of a British Ambassador would not know anything about it all.

He paused for effect.

'And meanwhile, Your Highness, to show what you think of the British Ambassador and his calls for retrenchment, how about giving another of your spectacular Balls in the Throne Room of the Dolmabahcheh Palace with your harem known to be watching unseen, high-up from behind the screens?'

'Yes, why not?' enthused the normally taciturn Sultan. He thought for a moment. 'Right!'

Meanwhile, Agha Ali's mind had been racing. The Sultan had said what he wanted: a well-educated English girl! And money was no object! Ali's cunning mind was racing. How was he going find a suitable girl without causing a scandal before one of his rival Aghas found one?

He remembered a certain conversation he had had with one of his women slave dealer friends with international contacts... She was very shortly expecting delivery from Marseilles of an interesting well-educated European girl. He had even seen her photograph. She looked very suitable: a pretty, innocent-looking, English-looking girl with a good figure.

Yes, he decided, he must quickly go and find out what nationality the girl was. If, by any chance, she was English... well! He'd certainly steal a march over his rival eunuch overseers. Yes indeed!

Chapter 9 - Jane's First Encouner with the Whip

Meanwhile, in a certain secluded house in the old quarter of Constantinople, Jane was spending a horrible hour. She tried to open the door, she shook the bars on the window, she called out and she knocked on the walls... all without any effect. She was, she realised, just a poor helpless young girl at the mercy of this terrifying Turkish woman. My God! My God!

And her awful threat of the whip! She feared that more than anything else. Even as a little girl, she had been terrified of corporal punishment, ever since one her friends, maltreated by a wicked aunt, had told her how she had been beaten and how much it had hurt. Oh Holy Mother of God, save me, save me, she cried, thinking back to the prayers that the nuns had taught her. What have I done to be so unhappy?

But perhaps, she thought, the woman had simply wanted to frighten her and turn her into a docile little plaything. Perhaps...

Suddenly Jane heard the key in the door and Fazileh-hanum entered. Jane tried to ignore her, but her unpleasant voice made Jane turn towards her.

'Well, child,' she muttered in her guttural French, 'I've come to introduce you to a nice gentleman who is anxious to get to know you.'

Jane stood with her back against the bed, determined to defend her virtue.

'Ha!' the woman sniggered. 'He's not what you think. Not yet! Your virginity has first to be checked and certified - and a certain little operation first needs to be carried out.'

'What!' Jane cried. 'What operation? How dare you talk to me like this!'

'And I advise you, young lady, to keep a respectful tongue in your head and be nice and eager to please,' replied the woman grimly. 'If not, the gentleman I spoke to you about will have to teach you a little lesson in politeness. Look! Here he is!'

From behind her back she produced a whip. Jane tried to ignore it, but, horrified, she simply could not take her eyes off the length of well-oiled pleated black leather that the woman was making snake to and fro whilst she watched the girl out of the corner of her eye.

'Isn't he lovely?' she said finally. 'So nice and pliable!'

She raised the short black handle in the air and suddenly cracked the whip, making Jane jump with fear.

'Don't be so frightened, Jane,' she laughed cruelly. 'He hasn't come for you just yet! But in case you think I'm not serious, I'd like you to come with me.'

'Why?' Jane asked nervously. 'What to do?'

'Why, just to see a little demonstration of what seems to frighten you so much. Hurry! I'm not going to say it again.'

Jane's first instinct was to refuse to move, but the another crack of the whip killed her brave resolve. She meekly followed the woman out of the room and down a dark, but whitewashed corridor. Perhaps she might find a way of escaping. But her hopes were in vain. There were no windows, just several half open doors, which let in lines of bright sunlight.

Through one doorway, a little wider open than the others, she glimpsed the brilliant blue sky, with a distant view and of darker blue sea that must she realised be the Bosphorus. A steamship was going along it. Freedom was so near and yet so far.

The room they entered was the first one that Jane had ever seen decorated in the oriental style. There was little furniture, just a sofa that ran almost right round the room and some small fretwork tables, some carpets on the floor, a few hangings on the wall and a brass lamp hanging from the ceiling. At the end of the room was a window covered by a wooden screen which let in little arrows of bright sunlight.

Jane saw that three women were there waiting for her. Two were large Negresses with hard faces and the third was a young white woman of about twenty or twenty-five. The Negresses were dressed in long European style dresses, but the girl was dressed in Eastern-style baggy pink satin pantaloons and a matching loose satin blouse. Jane would later learn that her blonde hair and dark eyes were typical of girls who came from the Caucasian provinces of the Turkish Empire.

The two Negresses spoke to Jane's jailer in a language she did not understand. Then one of them turned to Jane.

'You never seen a girl whipped, eh?' she said in broken French.

'Certainly not,' said Jane coldly. 'In England women are treated with respect, not cruelty.'

The Negress and the other two women began to laugh in a nasty menacing way.

'You now make fuss if this lazy white slave punished,' said the other Negress, again in broken French, 'but what you say if you see white slave girl whipped with corbash? You know what is corbash?'

'No,' stammered Jane with a shiver.

The Negress pulled out from below a cushion a strange sort of whip. It was longer, wider and thicker than the whip that Fazileh-hanum had showed her earlier and was made from one piece of leather. It was black and flexible, with a sharp point - terrifying to see.

'You see corbash!' said the Negress. 'He hippopotamus hide. He hurts! You'd better try not having him. You look at Nasima. She also just a slave - like you. She knows corbash well.'

Jane saw that the young woman who up till now had been quite impassive was now looking at the awful corbash with horror.

'This is not real!' cried Jane. 'No one would so cruel as to beat a woman with that, even she was a slave.'

'Ha! Nasima get corbash last week,' replied the first Negress with a grin. 'She get six strokes on bottom and two between legs. She just scream and scream!'

Jane was trembling all over and felt she was about to burst into tears, when suddenly Fazileh-hanum spoke.

'Enough talk! I brought the English girl here so that she could see what happens when I order a woman to be beaten. So let's get on with it!'

One of the Negresses gave an order to Nasima. Obediently, she jumped up and nervously began to unbutton her blouse.

'Stop it!' Jane begged. 'Please don't thrash this poor girl just because of me. Please!'

'So you'll be a good little girl?' asked Fazileh-hanum. 'You'll do what you're told?'

The woman looked at Jane harshly. Jane felt very frightened. She could feel her body tensing up as she tried to reply.

'Well... yes... but there are certain things that...'

'Well nothing!' replied the woman. 'I can see that you still need to see a girl of your own age being punished. You'll learn more from that than any amount of talk.'

Meanwhile, Nasima had taken off her blouse, disclosing delicate white shoulders and an opulent bosom. At least, Jane thought, the poor girl was going to beaten on her shoulders and not suffer the indignity of having her baggy trousers pulled down to bare her bottom. The first Negress seemed to have read her thoughts. She gave the girl another order and she slipped out of her pantaloons, baring her cheeks.

Jane gasped in horror for there right across the girl's plump bottom were still the distinctive marks of six strokes of the dreaded corbash.

'Yes, you now see,' laughed the Negress cruelly, 'what white woman's skin look like after beating. Turkish Masters much enjoy seeing see marks of cane or whip on white slave girls' bottoms.'

Again Jane gasped. But the stripes on the girl's bottom were not all, for she had been depilated - completely and shamefully depilated.

'Yes,' added the second Negress, noticing Jane's look, 'slave girls always kept depilated.'

'And,' cut in the other Negress, 'just you remember... although this time we now going to whip Nasima on shoulders... virgins always beaten on bottom - on bare bottom! Maybe you soon feel that!'

She put her hand under Jane's dress, making her jump away.

'Don't touch me,' Jane screamed, 'you horrible woman!'

The Negress just shrugged her shoulders and then, reluctantly putting down the corbash and, taking the whip from Fazileh-hanum, went up to the young woman who was standing quite still as if petrified.

She gave an order and Nasima, like a rabbit hypnotised by a stoat, went over to where two iron manacles were hanging from the ceiling. She raised her hands high above her head and one Negress quickly fastened the manacles round her wrists, whilst the other fastened her ankles wide apart to rings in the floor. She was now held helpless.

Then the first Negress then went to the side of the room and pulled down a cord that slightly raised the manacles. She adjusted the cord and then tied it to a hook on the wall, leaving the girl standing on tip-toe, her body and her parted legs strained upwards.

'That's proper position for beating on shoulders' explained the second Negress to Jane. 'You soon learn!'

Up to then, Jane had not been sure that such a dreadful and barbarous punishment was really going to take place. But there was no denying it now, with the girl bared and tied for punishment and the first Negress waving the terrible whip. Suddenly, horrified at what was about to happen, Jane flew at the Negress and seized her wrists with all the strength in her body.

'No! No!' she cried, 'don't do it! Beat me, if you want, but don't beat this poor girl who has done nothing.'

Laughing, the other Negress quickly seized Jane's arms and, despite her writhing, soon held her still. Then the two of them forced her over to where two other manacles were hanging from the ceiling, just in front of Nasima. They forced her arms up and snapped the manacles round her wrists. She was now as helpless as Nasima.

Then they undid her blouse. Moments later she, too, was naked to the waist. Jane felt desperately ashamed, but her jailer ran her hands approvingly over Jane's firm young breasts.

'Agha Ali like see these,' she murmured. Jane gasped. Who was Agha Ali? Could he be something to do with the Imperial Harem that the woman had talked about?

But her shame was not yet over for Fazileh-hanum said something to the second Negress, and moments later Jane's skirt her shift and her drawers were also all lying on the floor. Jane too was now stark naked. How she longed to cover herself with her hands! But the manacles held them firmly above her head.

Then the first Negress patted Jane's bottom

'Now you imagine what corbash would be like here,' she laughed, making Jane tremble at the mere idea.

'Or here between legs,' said the other.

Fazileh-hanum then said something to the two women who grinned and then fastened Jane's ankles wide apart like those Nasima.

Whip in hand, one of them now went behind Nasima. Out of the corner of her eye Jane saw her raise her whip. She closed her eyes so as not see it fall, but nothing happened. She opened her eyes and just at that very moment there was a sudden crack, and with an accuracy obviously born of much practice the whip fell neatly across the white shoulders of the young woman.

Jane gave a cry which was echoed by a scream from Nasima. The three older women all grinned as they watched the two young women now tugging desperately at their wrist manacles. Coldly Fazileh-hanum pointed to the long mark left on Nasima's shoulders.

'Just think,' she said, running her hands over Jane's equally naked shoulders and round towards her quivering breasts, 'what the whip would feel like here? And my friends are not yet using the corbash - only the whip. And only gently. Think what it would like to have a really hard stroke of the corbash from a big, burly, great Negro eunuch. They all hate Europeans and really enjoy beating a white Christian girl.'

Jane shuddered. A eunuch? She remembered how at the convent she and Helen had taken advantage of the absence of the nun in charge of their class to look up that word and had learned all about eunuchs. She had felt sorry for them then, but this Turkish woman's description of them had hardly fitted her image of weak and pitiful creatures.

But such thoughts were then driven out of her mind by the woman nodding to the Negress. Immediately another stroke of the whip fell, and there was another frantic cry from Nasima. My God, Jane thought, am I going to get the next stroke?

She could not take her eyes off the whip as the Negress made it snake along the floor and then slowly raised it. The women laughed and the third stroke fell across Nasima's shoulders to be followed by another scream.

Nasima was then released. Still naked and sobbing, she crouched on the floor, rubbing her shoulders to ease the pain.

'That just a little punishment,' said the first Negress to Jane. 'You lucky if you only get little punishment like that too.'

Fazileh-hanum now said something to the two Negresses, who again grinned. One of them slightly eased the cord holding Jane's manacles taut.

The other Negress gave her a sharp tap on her bottom with the whip. 'Bend knees!' she ordered. Jane was too frightened not to obey.

'And thrust out belly!' ordered the other woman, sitting herself down on a stool right in front of Jane, who then blushed as her beauty lips were parted. Moments later she gave a cry as she felt the woman's hands probing inside her.

'Yes, she's still a virgin,' the Negress reported.

Fazileh-hanum clapped her hands with delight.

'You'll be sold for a good price,' she told the appalled Jane. 'But first we must get you ready for inspection.'

She said something to the women who again grinned. Jane saw one of them go to a corner of the room where a pot of something was simmering on a small stove. She watched, horrified, as the woman returned with the pot in her hand and held it out to Fazileh-hanum who picked up a large wooden spoon, dipped it into the pot and lifted it out full of a sort of sticky paste. She nodded her approval and handed it back.

'Thrust belly forward!' she ordered.

Then she bent down over Jane's proffered mound and began to smear the hot paste over her hair. Jane started as she felt the heat working its way down past her hair to her skin but the straps held her legs tight.

Worse was to follow, for the Negress dipped the wooden spoon back into the pot and, holding Jane's virginal little beauty lips apart with one hand, with the other she smeared the still hot paste all along the line of the lips. Then, satisfied, she stood back to allow it to cool and solidify and started to talk in some strange language to her companion.

Then after several minutes, she reached down.

'Hold her tight!' she warned. Then, with an experienced hand, she ripped off the paste.

Jane screamed. Then she felt the woman's hand running over her mound and down her lips. There was a pause and then the whole process was repeated. Fazileh-hanum stepped forward and nodded her approval as she ran her hand over Jane's now smooth and almost hairless mound and beauty lips.

'Pluck out the remaining hairs,' she ordered and left the room.

By the time she returned, quarter of an hour later, Jane was quite hairless.

'Yes,' she laughed, 'a nice smooth little Christian virgin, ready for a rich Pasha's enjoyment - unless Agha Ali intervenes first.'

Again Jane did not understand what she meant. Who was this Agha Ali? However, the Negresses were already unfastening her wrists and ankles. Looking in a mirror Jane was shocked to see that her intimacies were now as hairless as those of a newborn babe.

The obviously delighted Fazileh-hanum pointed to a pair of silken trousers and a blouse lying on the sofa. 'Put these on!' she ordered, throwing Jane's own clothes, her best clothes, into the corner of the room. 'You won't need these here. Slave girls aren't entitled to wear European clothes.'

Too terrified to protest and anxious to put on anything to hide her nakedness, Jane ran over to the sofa. She saw that unlike Nasima's satin pantaloons, these were of silk and were shamefully transparent. So too was the blouse. Oh, no! She couldn't. She just couldn't.

Fazileh-hanum called out something to the first Negress. Jane saw her coming towards her with the whip raised. Hastily she pulled on the trousers and put on the blouse. Horrified, she saw her body clearly through the material. But anything, yes anything, was better than the whip!

Fazileh-hanum led Jane from the room and along the corridor back to her own bare room, holding her firmly by the arm. Jane heard the key turn in the lock as she flung herself on the bed and wept - more horrified than ever.

So she really was in the hands of Turkish slave dealers - at the mercy of their whips. And what dreadful whips they were! How could poor girls like Nasima and herself be treated in such a dreadful way? But even worse was the thought that a black man was coming to inspect her! And to check her virginity! The Negresses were bad enough but a man...

How perfectly dreadful. She would die of shame.

Chapter 10 - The Sultan's Anger is Assuaged

Agha Ali's reverie was interrupted by the Sultan's still angry voice.

'Well Agha Ali, what have you now got to offer me to make up for the Ambassador's insults - even if you can't yet offer me an English girl?'

Smiling, Ali led the way to an alcove and pulled back the curtain to disclose three very similar beautifully made-up, and frightened-looking, mousy-haired white girls, chained together by the neck and standing up silently on a low platform.

They were not wearing the usual green skimpy harem dress of Agha Ali's Orta but, as a change, long embroidered green caftans with similarly embroidered little green caps perched on the side of their heads. From these little caps a row of pearls hung across each of their foreheads - one of Ali's touches.

Like all Christian girls when displayed to the Sultan, they had had to step over their manacles so that their hands were held helpless behind their backs - to prevent them from trying to harm their Imperial Master.

'You will remember these eighteen year-old Romanian ones, Your Highness,' murmured Ali. 'A happy young bride and her two betrothed bridesmaids, captured by a raiding party of slave dealers, on the eve of the marriage and spirited away across the Turkish border to be offered in secrecy to the Imperial Harem.'

He reached forward and unfastened the buttons of the caftans on their shoulders, slipping them down to reveal slim waists and full breasts whose nipples were linked with little gold chains. He was particularly proud of having bought these three very similar white girls for his Orta, even though they weren't proper blondes. Although such a unique multiple acquisition had made a serious hole in his annual budget, he was confident that a delighted Sultan would soon reimburse him. The had certainly aroused the jealous anger of his rival Aghas and especially of his *bête noire* Agha Turki, who as the Commander of the Blue Orta of Greek girls was his particular rival.

'Wriggle!' muttered Agha Ali angrily. These girls should have been wriggling their bodies invitingly from the very start - as he had given orders that they were to be made to practice. Instead they were just standing there, lifeless. That was no way to attract the attention of a jaded Sultan.

'Wriggle,' he again whispered. But to no avail.

He turned to the Sultan, smiling to hide his inward anger.

'You will remember, Your Highness, that last month each of them in turn had been taken out of the Court of Innocent Virgins on different afternoons and chained down on their backs to offer their virginities to Your Highness - their precious virginities that they had been so carefully keeping for their betrothed, but which they were now helpless to prevent the Representative of Allah on Earth from taking.'

'Ah, yes,' smiled the Sultan, forgetting for the moment the insults he had just endured from the British Ambassador. 'They were a splendid find - and taking the virginities of these formerly betrothed Christian girls was indeed very enjoyable - a very exciting feeling. Their acquisition did you great credit, Agha Ali Effendi.'

Agha Ali bowed. The addition of the title Effendi after his name, somewhat similar to the English Esquire, was indeed a sign of the Sultan's favour.

Ali had come a long way since, like the other eunuchs in the Imperial Harem, he had been castrated by slavers in his native village in the Soudan and brought to Constantinople where he had been acquired for the Imperial Harem. Here his intelligence and native cunning, and his firmness in dealing with recalcitrant Christian women, had been noticed by the Kizlar Aghasi and had earned him quick promotion.

He remembered with pride how, the previous month, he had walked ahead of the Sultan's carriage in the weekly procession to the mosque Friday's prayers, proudly displaying to cheering crowds the signs of the Sultan's continuing virility: the single sheet that showed the virgin blood stains of the three Romanian girls taken by the Sultan. It was a sight that made the onlookers proud of their Sultan, especially as a cross in the corner of the sheet showed that the virgins had been abducted Christian girls.

'Serve the infidels right!' the crowd had shouted. 'Long live our virile Sultan!'

The Kizlar Aghasi, pleased by the Sultan's praise for his protégée, had also been alarmed by the lifelessness of the Romanian girls.

'Agha Ali, Agha Ali Effendi,' he said, anxious to support his subordinate, 'has now completed the disciplinary training of these three girls and they are ready as a team to pleasure their Master. Their rear entrances have been well stretched and they have been kept on a liquid diet. I am sure that now, perhaps with just a little encouragement from the cane, they will be only too anxious to show you how they can offer you exquisite delight there, too.'

He nodded to Ali who made the blushing girls turn round. He then dropped their caftans to their ankles, displaying their well rounded bottoms, across which were the marks of the cane - a sign of

Agha Ali's "disciplinary training". Such marks were, Agha Ali knew, something that the Sultan found arousing - particularly on a white Christian slave girl.

But the marks of the cane were not all, for on the girls' right cheeks glistened the brand marks of the Imperial Harem. The Kizlar Aghasi knew well the Sultan's predilection, like many Turks, for enjoying taking a horrified slavegirl up her bottom - especially if she was a Christian girl not used to such goings-on. Therefore, once the Sultan had taken a girl's virginity, the Kizlar Aghasi liked to have a girl branded on the bottom so that her Master would be further aroused by seeing it each time she was paraded naked up and down in front of him - and again each time he sodomised her.

Even the four Kadins still bore the degrading brand of their Master on the right cheek of their bottoms - as a reminder that they had once been humble concubines. Furthermore if the Sultan later munificently gave a girl away to a particularly deserving or favourite Bey or Pasha, then she would still be bearing the Imperial brand in her new harem - a constant reminder to her new Master of the Sultan's generosity.

'Wriggle your bottoms,' muttered Agha Ali, trying to stimulate such life into this precious team of girls. But they just stood there like dummies. My God, thought Agha Ali, they're going to get a beating after this. He wasn't going to stand for such disobedience.

'Umm!' murmured the Sultan. Having all three Romanian girls brought to his bed together would certainly make an interesting evening. But he could not help thinking that they looked a bit dull and lifeless.

'Or alternatively,' came a sudden interruption from a new high pitched voice, 'Your Highness might be more interested in this.'

The voice was that of Agha Turki, one of Ali's great rivals and the Commander of the Blue and White Orta of Greek girls. He had suddenly appeared. By rights he should not have done so as his Orta was not on duty that day, but it was a rule that the Kizlar Aghasi did not always enforce - if it resulted in the Sultan being pleased with the sudden offer of a new girl.

Agha Turki was almost as grossly fat as the Kizlar Aghasi himself. He glanced contemptuously at Agha Ali and his three young Romanian girls and then led the way across to a different alcove. He pulled back the curtain of this alcove to display a single dark haired young woman - chained by the neck to a ring in the wall. Her hands were manacled behind her back, her legs chained wide apart and she was gagged with a black leather muzzle.

She was wearing the erotic looking traditional blue and white coloured harem dress of a slavegirl of Agha Turki's Greek Orta. Blue and white stripes made up the flag of the small independent Greece that had obtained its freedom after a bitter war against its Turkish overlords earlier in the 19th Century. But northern Greece and many of the Aegean islands, like Crete, were still held down under a ruthlessly imposed Turkish rule. By dressing his enslaved Greek concubines in the national colours of the free Greece, the Sultan was cruelly emphasising to them their own loss of freedom.

'Alternatively,' Agha Turki repeated, to Aki's silent rage, 'Your Highness might like this Greek woman, Helene, the wife of rebel in Crete.'

Ali swallowed his anger and disappointment as Turki slowly stripped this Greek woman for the Sultan's inspection. He had been so sure that the Sultan would eagerly choose his three Romanian girls and now that wretched Turki was trying to steal is thunder with some damn Greek woman.

However, even Ali had to admit that Helene was a lovely young woman with the mature body that often appealed to the jaded Sultan. Her eyes were flashing above her muzzle and angry little moans of protest could be heard coming out from under it. No wonder that Agha Turki had not wanted to risk this angry young Christian woman, a mere infidel, committing the sacrilege of insulting the Sultan, the Shadow of Allah on Earth. The penalty for that was death - and what financial gain would he get from that?

'I thought it prudent, Your Highness,' Turki explained, 'to display her gagged and chained, lest she might be tempted to insult or kick Your Highness. The woman is not fully broken in nor, as a married Christian girl, is she yet fully appreciative of the great honour of being offered to the Representative of Allah on Earth for his pleasure.'

The Sultan nodded in approval. Used to girls reduced to subservience, an untamed and resentful married Christian woman always particularly aroused his jaded interest. He reached forward and lifted up a full firm breast. 'Age?' he asked laconically.

'Thirty, Your Highness,' replied Agha Turki.

'A widow?'

'No yet, Your Highness. Her infidel dog of a young rebellious Christian husband was caught plotting a revolt against Your Highness in Crete. As a punishment, the Governor of Crete ordered that he be bastinadoed and imprisoned whilst his beautiful wife, the apple of his eye, was be sent to Your Highness as a present.'

'Ah!' The Sultan smiled, his former interest in the three Romanian girls fading fast. He particularly enjoyed taking the wives of Christian dissidents, keeping them in his harem under the cruel control of his black eunuchs.

'And have you interrogated her to find out whether she formerly enjoyed regular sex with her husband?

'Yes, Your Highness - and she did.'

Better and better, thought the Sultan, she would feel all the more her forthcoming enforced frustration and dedication to the sensual desires of her new Master.

'Well, I presume she has now been cut?'

It was considered seemly for Christian slavegirls to feel any pleasure themselves as they were made to arouse their Turkish owners. Yet it made a girl all the more desperate to be chosen by her Master for his bed. Only when a cut girl was actually penetrated, in the normal Western way, would she be able to feel any pleasure herself - and even then she would not dare for fear of the attending young eunuch's cane to climax without permission.

She would of course soon be desperate to ease her frustration by finding a way of secretly satisfying herself with an artificial manhood. The eunuchs always therefore made sure that no such rubber or ivory dildos were introduced into the harem amongst the wares offered by visiting tradeswomen. They even ensured that bananas and cucumbers were always sliced up before being served in the harem.

The Sultan greatly enjoyed the thought of them being kept frustrated, especially in the case of a married Christian woman, used to regular sexual pleasure with her husband, like this Greek Helene. Hence the Sultan's question.

'Of course, Your Highness. And at the same time, as you can see, the unsightly protruding inner lips have been trimmed back. Look, Your Highness!'

Ignoring Helene's moans of protest and vain attempts to pull away from him, Agha Turki now reached forward and ran his hands over her belly and down between her parted legs and over her now depilated and hairless beauty lips which were now touching each other with no sign of the inner lips.

'Yes, they now make a pleasing sight,' commented the Sultan.

Agha Turki then parted the lips. There was no sign of the clitoris - just a tiny scar.

Better and better, the Sultan was thinking as, stroking his chin with one hand, he reached forward with the other to touch the little scar - as if to make sure that there was no response.

'And,' went on the Sultan, his eyes gleaming, 'have her young husband brought over from Crete to be incarcerated chained in the harem dungeons - where she can be taken to see him before being made to submit again to my will. '

Agha Turki gave a cruel laugh.

'Your Highness, the husband is already locked up down below!'

'Aha!' cried the Sultan. 'Well done, Agha Turki... Well done indeed, Agha Turki Effendi. Excellent!'

He paused for a moment whilst like Agha Ali earlier on, Agha Turki smiled happily at the accolade of being called an Effendi by the Sultan himself.

'Well, in that case,' ordered the Sultan, all thoughts of the three Romanian girls now completely brushed aside, 'have her taken straight down to my dungeons - and I'll come with you to enjoy the sight of the rebellious husband's helpless chagrin as you tell him she about to be taken by me, his Ruler. And then you can bring her, still gagged and manacled, to my bedroom in an hour's time.'

It was an order that made Agha Ali silently suck his teeth with anger.

Turki was smirking with pleasure and gave Ali a triumphant glance.

The Kizlar Aghasi smiled to himself. This rivalry between the Aghas ensured a constant supply of beautiful young white creatures for the well satisfied Sultan - and thus reinforced the security of his own position, quite apart from that of the Aghas concerned.

Ali raised his eyes to the ceiling in despair. Clearly, the Sultan was going to be absorbed by humiliating this young Greek couple -

and the wretched Turki's star would be well and truly in the ascendant.

'Then,' went on the Sultan, 'after I have enjoyed taking her several times, I think she might then well be a good candidate for a curved belly. It would be amusing to see the wife of a rebel mated with my Black Guards and undergoing a forced motherhood.'

This remark was greeted with enthusiasm by Turki. There was an old Turkish saying: "To teach Christian dogs a lesson, put the wives of rebellious Christians to your black slaves."

'And even more amusing to have her mounted by my Black Guards in front of her beloved rebel of a former husband - and then later to make her display her well curved belly to him.'

Agha Turki remembered his friend Agha Selim of the Syrian Orta, and Madeleine his French former governess. Despite her age she was turning out to be very profitable investment for Selim. Perhaps this older married girl from Crete would be an equally profitable investment for him, more than repaying what he had paid for her.

'Perhaps,' he whispered suggestively, 'Your Highness might like to see this Greek married slave mated at the same time as my colleague Agha Selim's Frenchwoman.'

'Umm!' murmured the Sultan, evidently taken by the idea.

'Certainly,' murmured the shrewd Kizlar Aghasi, 'they would then make a fine pair paraded naked for Your Highness with their identically curved bellies.'

'And,' added Agha Turki with a little cruel laugh, 'both commiserating with each other, when they first felt their unwanted progeny kicking.'

The Sultan smiled.

'Perhaps,' whispered the Kizlar Aghasi, 'my other subordinate, the Agha of the Curved Bellies, might even be able to arrange that they delivered their progeny simultaneously, wriggling alongside each other on the special harem double birthing chair, with the Agha using his whip to hurry things along.'

Again the Sultan smiled.

Oh yes, Agha Turki was thinking, the prospect of such a final spectacle and meanwhile the almost daily display to the Sultan of the two sobbing Christian women with their identical and increasingly curved white bellies, would certainly focus the attention of the

Sultan onto his Greek and Syrian Ortas. Yes, it would be one in the eye to the Balkan Orta of his principal rival, that damned Agha Ali.

Curse it, Agha Ali, was thinking. Unless he could step in with something else, the humiliation of this pretty young wife of a rebel is going to be the centre of the Sultan's attention for some time to come - instead of his three Romanian girls. And the degradation of this young white husband and wife would doubtless earn that damned Turki numerous bonuses from the delighted Sultan - bonuses that might otherwise have been coming to him.

Ali cursed to himself again as he thought how the Sultan, knowing how his loyal Moslem Turkish subjects hated the Greeks, would see to it that the story of the mating of the beautiful wife of a Greek rebel with one of the Sultan's huge Black Guards was widely told in the bazaars throughout the Ottoman Empire. Not only would this boost the popularity of the Sultan but would also intimidate other would-be Christian rebels.

He remembered how after a recent revolt in one of the Christian Balkan provinces, the bazaars had been full of the story of how the wife of the leading dissident had been captured and brought to the Sultan. Shortly after he had enjoyed her, the Kizlar Aghasi had reported that she was ready to conceive. She had then been chained, kneeling down naked on all fours before the Sultan. Then placing his foot on her neck and holding out his hand for her to lick humbly, the Sultan had given his permission for the mating to begin.

Three specially selected and masked members of the Sultan's Black Guards had then been brought in. The woman's overseer had used his cane to make her arouse each Black Guard in turn with her mouth and tongue. Then each Black Guard had mounted her.

Moreover, she had been further degraded, still chained down on all fours in front of the Sultan, by having to pleasure the Sultan by taking the Imperial Manhood into her mouth, whilst simultaneously being penetrated from behind by the Black Guards. It had amused the Sultan to climax into her mouth just as the fertilising seed of the last Black Guards was flooding up inside her from behind.

With her head kept down and the semen of three potent Black Guards competing to make her conceive, there had no chance of her escaping her fate - and soon drawings of her with a well-curved belly had begun to circulate. It had been a fine piece of propaganda and one that would undoubtedly be repeated about this Greek woman...

Ali's mind was in turmoil. There was, however, one bright hope. If the girl that his friendly slave dealer was expecting by boat from Marseilles was in fact English... well, then in view of what the Sultan had said about getting hold of an English girl for his harem... he'd soon wipe that smirk off Agha Turki's face.

She should have arrived by now. If she was English then he must go and see her without delay. He didn't want any one else snapping her up. But he must be careful not to appear too keen to buy her or the woman slave dealer would put up the girl's price - and buying those three Romanian girls had made a big hole in his budget for purchasing new concubines.

How they had let him down! By Allah, he swore to himself, they're going to get the full twenty-five strokes of his cane. He'd soon have them screaming to be allowed to wriggle their bodies properly again in front of the Sultan.

But meanwhile this possible English girl was more important. A young English girl locked up in the Court of Innocent Virgins and awaiting deflowering would certainly distract the Sultan's attention away from this from Greek woman.

Chapter 11 - Jane Already Has a Possible Buyer

That evening Jane again heard the key in the door. She was trembling all over as her jailer entered.

'Stand up when I enter,' she ordered, 'unless you want the whip.'

Scared stiff, Jane jumped up off the bed. The woman looked her over. Jane felt desperately ashamed at the transparency of her new clothes, and tried to hide herself with her hands.

'Yes, not bad, and much better without all that hair - and just as well as a very important old business friend of mine, a very important one, the Agha Ali that I mentioned earlier has just sent word that he is coming to inspect you for his Master tomorrow. Yes tomorrow! He's a very senior black eunuch in Imperial Harem. I had earlier sent him your photograph and he seems very interested in buying you.'

Inspect me for his Master? A senior black eunuch interested in buying me? Oh my God, thought Jane. And what was that about a photograph? What photograph, Jane wondered? But the woman's next words drove it out of her mind.

'He'll want to check your virginity for himself. And if he finds that you've lied to me and the Negresses were wrong, then I'll have you given the corbash by them.'

Terrified of the threat of the corbash, Jane again Jane protested her innocence.

'Good. In that case, slave, with your figure you're now going Allah willing to earn me a fortune - before you've even been really placed on the market or properly prepared!'

Chapter 12 - Helen Enjoys the High Life and Learns About Harems

10th May

Oh, I've been having such a wonderful time. So much so that, I'm afraid, I've quite deserted my poor diary.

I've been leading a life of gaiety and enjoyment such as I've never come across before. I just wish Jane could have been here to share it - and for us to have explored more of that secret pleasure we had together on that wonderful last day at school. How shocked the nuns would have been if they had known.

Every day Maria would take me with her, shopping in the gorgeous French shops, or to see the magnificent mosques, followed by a siesta in the afternoon - with further parties in the evening.

Last weekend we drove out to spend a couple of days at the country house of Maria's family some ten miles up the Bosphorus at Tarabya.

Here, amidst green parks sloping down to the blue waters of the Bosphorus, the ambassadors of the Great Powers, Britain, France, Germany, Russia, Austria and Italy all have their summer residences: white painted wooden yalis on the water's edge. Lying moored off these splendid villas lay each Power's own naval gunboat.

In the afternoons the quay at Tarabya became a highly cosmopolitan promenade with diplomats, journalists, bankers, from both all over Europe and officials of the Ottoman Empire itself, all exchanging gossip and news. But I couldn't help noticing that it was also the place where the bright young things and bored wives and their aspiring lovers flirted and paraded before going on to tennis matches and polo tournaments - or even, for the quite large number of young English merchants, bankers and diplomats, a game of cricket.

In the evenings there were dances or balls, or if there was no ball then the young lovers and would-be lovers would embark in kayiks and would be joined by other kayiks from the various lit up villages and yalis that dotted both the Asian and European shores of the mile wide Bosphorus. Some kayiks would carry musicians and others food and all together they were drift slowly drift down the flat calm Bosphorus, calling in at the yalis of friends or just enjoying the evening's delights.

Maria told me that sometimes there were as many as a thousand kayiks drifting down the beautiful twenty-mile strip of water surrounded by rolling hills and woods. Sometimes they even drifted down the Bosphorus until dawn, overwhelmed by the beauty of the night and sound of music.

I've been constantly running into David Lyons, the handsome young naval officer I saw on that first evening on the Bosphorus. He is charming and very attentive. For the first time in my life, I feel that I am falling in love. Of course I love Jane but, I feel, this is different. He's a man!

How sad that I'm only here for a few more weeks. But perhaps Maria's parents, who seem very pleased for Maria to have a sensible English companion, might ask me back again before too long...

12th May

I've been fascinated by the many vast new gleaming white marble palaces on the water's edge: the palaces of the Sultan, His Imperial Majesty, as he was officially termed, and of members of the royal family. The sheer size and splendour of the palaces, especially of the Sultan's own huge Dolmabahcheh Palace, is astonishing.

Every time I go down or back up the Bosphorus, this large palace down on the water's edge with its high white marble façade inevitably catches my eye. It had been built, Maria told me, only some fifty years before by the Sultan's father who wanted to out-do Buckingham Palace and Versailles.

They say it stretches almost a quarter of a mile along the shore of the Bosphorus and is believed to have over 300 rooms including several huge open drawing rooms, each decorated in an elaborate rococo style with gold leaf everywhere. Along the front of the palace a marble terrace is lapped by the blue waters of the sea, and in the centre of the terrace are the marble steps that form the Sultan's own landing stage.

I was astonished, the first time we were rowed past it, when Maria said that the half of it with the windows discreetly covered over with lattice work housed the mysterious Imperial Harem - and presumably the Sultan's own bedroom.

'But the harem quarters look huge!' I exclaimed.

'Well remember that it has to hold over a hundred concubines.'

'A hundred white women,' I repeated in astonishment.

'Yes and all their eunuch overseers.'

Maria also told me how the Sultan would occasionally invite the cream of Constantinople society to a magnificent ball given in the vast Throne Room. How civilised! Oh! If only he were to give another Ball before I have to go home.

However, Maria said this veneer of Western civilisation was only wafer thin for it was said that behind the lattice screens high up on the side of the Throne Room the Sultan's mainly white Christian slavegirls, carefully watched over by their eunuchs, would be peering down wistfully at the sight of the society with which they were forbidden to mix.

How envious they must be of those free women, dancing and flirting with men - for Maria says the eunuchs make sure that the only fair-skinned man who ever saw them, or whom they ever saw save at a distance, was their Master the Sultan.

They say that one small locked door, continually guarded day and night by eunuchs, links the two wings of the Dolmabahcheh and only the Sultan is allowed to pass through it. Hidden away from the outside world beyond this door is the Sultan's collection of beautiful white women, all kept secretly and anonymously locked up under the supervision of the Kizlar Aghasi and his assistant eunuchs.

How sad, Maria said, it must be for the women to peer wistfully out at the passing European steamships ships or look down at the marble terrace steps where Ambassadors and other important Westerners, calling on the Sultan, step out of their boats to be met by the Sultan's equerries. Yes, the free world was only a stone's throw away but for them it might as well be on a different planet.

Apparently, here and in the Sultan's new secluded and park-like Yildiz Palace, built up on a hill behind the Dolmabahcheh Palace, the eunuchs make sure that the women in their charge had no contact with this freer and Europeanised outside world. The only men with whom they were allowed to speak are large and powerful-looking men with the negroid features and the high pitched voices of eunuchs.

It's all getting more and more extraordinary. I have never heard of such things before.

13th May

I've noticed as we go up and down the Bosphorus that half the windows of each of the other palaces and yalis or villas down by the water's edge, are also mysteriously covered by a mixture of curved oriental-style stone tracery and wooden screens.

Maria says that each hides a strictly enclosed harem, each with its own white slave girls and eunuch guardians. The tracery and screens are to keep prying eyes out - and to prevent the slavegirls from escaping from their cruel Turkish Masters. How dreadful!

How many young white women would be sadly peering out through the screens for a glimpse of the nearby freedom that is so cruelly denied them by their Master's eunuchs. What a terrible culture the harem system here seems to be.

Maria says that, a Turk can have up to four wives and as many, mainly Christian, slavegirl concubines as he can afford. But even the wives are not really free to come and go unsupervised by eunuchs - and as for the concubines, the only man the eunuchs allow them to see close up or to talk to is their Master.

I must say I find all this casual talk of these harems and of the appalling life that goes on inside them to be very shocking. The nuns had never told us about such things. Are they really true?

Chapter 13 - Inspection

The next day, Jane again suddenly heard the key in the lock of her door.

Scared stiff, she saw Fazileh-hanum enter the room and silently beckon her to follow her. She was looking rather excited and Jane wondered what could be the reason.

'You have a visitor,' the woman told Jane, 'and so be on your best behaviour - or you'll get the corbash. Understand?

Terrified by this threat, Jane nodded.

Once again, the woman led Jane, still dressed in just her transparent trousers and blouse, down the corridor. Once again she had a glimpse of the distant Bosphorus. But, instead of going into the room in which Jane had seen poor Nasima being beaten, she led her on out into a deserted courtyard surrounded with colonnades.

But Jane had no time to look around, for the woman pushed her onto in a room in the corner of the courtyard. It was a large Turkish bathroom, delightfully cool and clean. The walls were covered with blue and white coloured tiles. In the centre of the similarly tiled floor was a raised small large pool, the bath itself - full of clean and inviting hot water. Beyond, that a Turkish carpet lay diagonally across the floor and in a corner was a mass of mattresses and cushions covered in material of every colour.

The whole room was bathed in a gentle light coming from beautifully coloured, opaque skylights let into the tiled ceilings. Like all Turkish Baths it was warm.

Jane saw that coming across the room to greet her, a smile on her lips, was a young woman. It was Nasima, the girl who had been so casually beaten in front of her. She seemed to have forgotten about it, but Jane felt her herself blushing at the shameful memory of all that had happened. But before she could gather her thoughts properly, she heard the harsh voice of Fazileh-hanum.

'Get into the bath, Jane. Hurry up! And you, Nasima, undress her, and get her ready for our potential buyer.'

As Nasima was about to slip down Jane's pantaloons, she saw two other figures sitting in a corner of the room. They were Negresses: the ones who had whipped Nasima. Their cruel eyes were fixed on Jane. She felt humiliated and frightened.

But then she noticed another figure, this time sitting quietly on a sofa behind the Negresses. She was highly embarrassed to see that by his dress he was a man, a man wearing a red fez cap like many of the men barely had time to notice on the quay when the ship arrived.

He was holding a little black bag - like a doctor's bag. But he was formally dressed in a black morning coat like an educated European.

She blushed at being half naked in front of a man. Indeed the sight of this man and the contrast with his European style formal dress and her own shamefully transparent slave girl dress horrified her. He turned and looked at her and she suddenly realised that he was a Negro and a jet black one at that. She had hardly ever seen a black man before. And evidently he was in a position of authority! Jane could not help trembling.

'That is Mr Ali who has come to inspect you,' whispered Fazileh-hanum. 'He's a very important person. So say good morning to him nicely.'

She was going to be inspected by this black man! Oh no! And to be half naked in front of him now! She felt so ashamed. She just could not a word. Horrified, she again tried to cover her body with her hands.

'Into the bath!' repeated the woman. 'And be quick about it.'

But Jane just stood there as if transfixed. The two Negresses and the Negro remained motionless.

'Obey her!' Nasima whispered encouragingly. She paused and then went on in her broken French. 'Take down pantaloons! Quick! Or they use whip.'

She pointed towards the two Negresses who had now come over to her. Horrified she saw that one of them was holding a whip - like the one they had used on her and Nasima. The lash was trailing along the floor. My God!

'Well?' the woman shouted. 'Are you going to strip? Yes or no?'

Jane saw that the Negro was watching her closely. 'No, not in front of him,' she cried out, pointing to the black man and trembling with a mixture of fear and indignation.

Before she could realise what was happening, one of the Negresses brought the whip across her right arm. It felt like a knife cutting into her flesh and she screamed with the pain. Then she felt another similar pain on the left shoulder. Again she screamed with the frightful pain.

'Take off your clothes,' ordered Fazileh-hanum, 'or I'll have you thrashed until they're cut into pieces - and probably your skin as well.

The Negress caught Jane with a third stroke of her whip, this time across her breasts. Jane fell forward, feeling as if she had been touched with a red hot iron.

'Take off blouse,' whispered Nasima. 'Whip naughty, hurt very much.'

The slavegirl undid the buttons of Jane's thin blouse. Jane did not stop her. All she could think of were the dreadful strokes of the whip. Then as the girl slipped the blouse off, Jane looked at her arms and down at her breasts. Horrified she saw that her lovely soft white skin was marked with three red lines.

Seeing the look on her face, Fazileh-hanum laughed.

'Good! With such a sensitive skin, a man would really enjoy watching you being given the whip.'

Nasima's hands were now on her trousers, undoing the buttons that held them up across her hips. Jane pushed her away, holding her trousers up with one hand.

'Still disobedient? Right!' She said something to the Negress who nodded and grinned. 'You're going to be given a stroke across the calves! And you, Nasima, pay attention!'

Nasima gave Jane a sympathetic look, and then Jane felt the awful thong whipping round her legs. The pain was so dreadful that she fell to her knees, her head in her hands. It was just what Fazileh-hanum had wanted and she snapped her fingers at Nasima, who quickly pulled Jane's pantaloons down to her knees and then off completely, leaving Jane kneeling on her floor quite naked.

'Now get into bath!'

Jane crawled to the bath and dropped in, too ashamed to look up. She felt Nasima's hands soaping her all over. The cool water eased her pain but not her shame. But there was more shame to follow, for she saw that the big black man was now standing by the bath, looking down at her with a detached almost professional way. He was huge and fat, with tribal scars on his cheeks. Under his fez, he seemed quite bald. She gasped in horror.

She saw he was carrying something in his hand, which he kept glancing at. It was a photograph. Suddenly she saw that it was the photograph of her that had been taken at the convent! She remembered that it had been sent by her guardian to the people in London who had apparently gone bankrupt. But how on earth had it come to be here?

Standing next to him and pointing down to her body was a smiling Fazileh-hanum. She was talking in Turkish and perhaps it was just as well that Jane did not understand a word of what was being said.

'His Highness would be pleased even if you had to pay an exceptionally large sum for such a rare and beautiful untouched flower!' said the woman slave dealer.

'Umm, I'm not sure about that! His Highness already has so many girls to choose from.'

'So many other girls perhaps,' protested Fazileh-hanum, 'but I'll warrant this one will be the only English one in the harem.'

What! Ali had difficulty in concealing his sheer exultation. So she was English! Hastily he controlled his feelings - or else the woman would put up the price.

'Bah!' he muttered, still trying to hide hiding his excitement. 'She's just one of the race who has so often deceived the Padishah - and who are constantly seeking to interfere in the way he rules his Christian provinces. They've already stolen Cyprus and now Egypt from him - the hateful infidels!'

'All the more reason for buying her!' The woman's voice took on a wheedling tone, though she was much nearer the truth than she realised. 'Think how he will reward you for enabling him to take the virginity of a proud English girl - and so take his revenge for all the humiliations he has suffered from the English. Think of his exquisite pleasure as he penetrates where not even an Englishman has ever penetrated before! Think of his gratitude to you for having so cleverly acquired such a rare flower for him to pluck... Just think, when was an educated and refined English girl's precious virginity last offered up to His Highness?'

'Well, perhaps it'll be worth just checking her virginity,' the big black man said in a bored voice.

The woman saw that her sales efforts were sinking home. 'Now get out and kneel on the cushion,' she ordered Jane.

Jane saw that Nasima had brought a large oriental cushion to where the two Negresses were standing. To emphasise the order one of them cracked her whip. Terrified, Jane jumped up and ran naked to the cushion. She saw that a smaller cushion had been placed next to the larger one.

Wonderingly, she knelt up on the large cushion, facing the smaller one, her hands covering her breasts. But the two Negresses pushed her head down so that she was now on all fours with her forehead touching the top of the small cushion and her hips forced up into the air.

To keep her there with her head down one of the Negresses now stood astride her neck, her powerful calves pressed tightly against Jane's cheeks, whilst the other held her wrists in a grip of iron.

'Open legs!' ordered Fazileh-hanum bringing her whip down across Jane's naked back. Again Jane screamed. But trembling with shame and fear, she opened her legs. Was her virginity going to be explored - this time by the Negro man? Oh my God! Could she run out of the room when they let go of her?

'Yes,' Fazileh-hanum continued, 'this girl's worth a fortune.'

The huge black man came behind Jane. She blushed with shame at the thought that she was wide open to his gaze.

'A little more open, please,' a strangely high pitched voice said from behind her in heavily accented French. Startled, Jane realised that it must be the voice of the Negro. How strange that such a huge brute of a man could have such a high-pitched voice.

Suddenly the whip came down again across her back.

'When Mr Ali asks you to open your legs, slave, you do so at once! Understand? At once!' cried the ruthless Fazileh-hanum. 'Now get those buttocks wide apart for his inspection... Wider!'

Terrified, back burning from the pain of the lash, Jane strained to do what her jailer was ordering.

'That's better,' came the same high-pitched voice.

Suddenly Jane felt hands. She looked down. Huge black hands were groping between her legs. No! No! How awful! Desperately, she tried to wriggle away, crying out in horrified protest. But the women held her tight. All she could do was to close her legs again. But as she did so the whip came down again across her back.

'You keep legs wide apart, little slave,' muttered Fazileh-hanum. 'Next time you get six strokes!'

'Lady must obey - and not speak,' came the whispered voice of Nasima. 'Or whip hurt pretty lady too much.'

Sobbing, Jane opened her legs again, wide apart. This time she tried to keep quite still and silent. But she simply could not help trembling all over when she felt the Negro's hands expertly part her beauty lips. Then she had to bite her lips as he felt upwards for her clitoris and began tickling it until he felt a good response - something that made Jane feel more ashamed than ever.

'She's not been cut!' complained Agha Ali, seeking to find fault, and so reduce the price of this English girl whom he really knew he must, at all cost, buy.

'She's only just arrived fresh from Europe,' came the protesting voice of Jane's captor.

'Nevertheless,' said Agha Ali, putting on a serious tine of voice, 'you know the Kizlar Aghasi's views about an infidel dog of a Christian slavegirl having enjoyment in the bed of the Sultan of Sultans, the Commander of the Faithful, the Caliph, the Lieutenant of Allah here on earth. For a mere Christian woman it is sufficient to have the great honour of being allowed to offer her body for the pleasure of the Shadow of Allah. It is not seemly for her also to have pleasure herself.'

He stopped for a moment to give greater emphasis to his words.

'That's why His Highness the Kizlar Aghasi has ordered that we should only to buy Christian girls who have been cut.'

'Then as you are such an experienced overseer of Christian girls,' said Fazileh-hanum flatteringly, 'why don't you cut her yourself? You saw how her clitoris swelled up when you aroused her - just snipping off the tip of it will prevent her feeling any pleasure - unless she is actually penetrated. Even then you can always train her not to show any pleasure. We could then keep her here for a day or two while the wound heals over and then deliver her to you, ready for display to His Highness.'

The Negro grunted. He'd done many a Christian girl and had confidence in his own ability.

'Well,' he said, 'maybe. But first I must just check her virginity.'

Jane was then horrified to feel his finger going gently up inside her. Suddenly it stopped.

'Yes, you're right - at least she is a virgin,' came the falsetto voice. 'That's something!'

Jane could have died of shame as she felt the black finger carefully examining her virginity. 'The hymen is intact and is a nice firm one worthy of being broken by the Imperial manhood - and she's beautifully tight! His Highness would enjoy that - forcing his way into her!'

'Yes, she's worth a fortune.'

'Um, I'm not sure she's really worth buying for my Orta,' replied Agha Ali in a sceptical tone of voice that hid his real excitement.

'Not worthy of the Imperial Harem? Of course she is. This pretty, slim but buxom English girl would be unique. Just have a look at her.'

She turned to Jane. 'Stand up girl and run round the room so that Agha Ali can have a good look at you.'

The order was emphasised by a crack of the whip.

Blushing, the naked but terrified Jane stood up. She, a respectable English girl, was being shown off to this awful Negro - like a filly being shown off at a horse sale. Oh the shame! She just couldn't do it.

But the whip cracked again.

'Go on girl - run! Head up!'

Fearfully, Jane began to run. Again the whip cracked, this time just behind her bare bottom.

'And now... raise your knees... Higher!' Again the whip cracked. 'Higher!'

Desperately Jane tried to obey. She could feel her long, well brushed blond hair swaying with her every step.

'And clasp your hands behind your neck! Prance!'

Now she had to lean back. It was a position, she realised, that thrust out her bouncing breasts.

'Go on! Prance right round the room again!'

Agha Ali was quietly assessing Jane. It was by no means the first time that a slave girl had been made to prance round for his benefit. Yes, he thought the breasts were nice and firm - and the girl's belly and bottom too. And her legs were long and slim. Quite apart from answering the Sultan's need for a well-educated young Englishwoman, she would be asset to his Orta. But if he appeared too keen, the woman would demand what she was undoubtedly worth.

'As you felt for yourself,' said the woman, 'she's still a virgin - a lovely innocent virgin to be offered up like a sacrifice to God's Lieutenant on Earth. And moreover an English virgin.'

'Well, perhaps I could come back tomorrow. But I'll only do her if you let me have her cheaply.'

'Of course Effendi,' the woman said ingratiatingly. Then she mentioned a high price.

'What!' cried Agha Ali, getting up as if to leave in disgust.

'Then make me an offer,' cried the woman.

Agha Ali offered her half what she had asked.

'What!' cried the slave dealer. 'I wouldn't sell an old toothless black grandmother for that!'

The bargaining continued.

Finally Agha Ali nodded his agreement. Then, looking around, he lowered his voice so that only Fazileh-hanum could hear.

'But if I am to recommend her purchase for such a sum, then...'

He paused. Quickly the cunning Fazileh-hanum cut in.

'I shall, of course, be paying you ten percent of the final purchase price.'

'Twenty!'

'Twenty per cent! You forget the considerable expense I have had to go to get an innocent English girl here. And the risks I have run! No! Twelve and that's my last word. Just remember that it'll be twelve per cent of a very large sum.'

'Fifteen!' murmured the huge Negro and turned to go. 'Or I shall say she is not a virgin.'

'Wait!' cried the woman, dismayed at the thought of losing the sale completely. 'Very well. Fifteen!'

The huge black man nodded.

'Oh, incidentally, he said, 'I like to cut from behind with the girl kneeling on all fours. You can see her clitoris better that way than when she's just lying on her back.'

Chapter 14 - Helen Learns More About Harems

14th May

I've been talking to Maria's old Negress nursemaid. She had once been a nursemaid in the harem of the last Sultan, the uncle of the present one. When he was deposed, his harem was relegated to the old Topkapi palace and she was allowed to leave and join the household of Maria's father. But she was still made welcome by in the present Sultan's harem by her former colleagues.

In the Imperial Harem, she explained, Negresses worked closely with their fellow African eunuchs in supervising the white concubines.

'But why are they always called black eunuchs?' I asked her.

'To distinguish them from the white eunuchs,'

'White eunuchs! Are they used in the harems as well?'

'Oh no! Never in the harem,' replied the former nursemaid, sounding quite shocked, in the fluent French she had first learned in the harem and then in Mavroyeni household.

She explained that only black eunuchs were used in the harems whilst white eunuch page boys are just used as personal attendants for their Masters, and later on as confidential clerks. The Turks think the concubines would twist white eunuchs round their little fingers, whereas they know they are terrified of black ones. The black eunuchs have a reputation of standing no nonsense from their white charges.

Moreover, I learned, whereas white eunuchs always seem to be thin and prematurely wizened, black eunuchs tend to be fat and strong. So they are really quite different. And whereas you don't see many white eunuchs these days, there are still plenty of black ones - in charge of the harems of all the rich Beys and Pashas as well as the Sultan's.

15th May

'But how about the Sultan?' I asked Maria's former nursemaid today as we were getting dressed for dinner. 'Doesn't he have any wives? I thought he was allowed four wives, four Sultanas!'

'Oh no!' she replied, going on to explain that traditionally the Sultan never married and that all the women in the Imperial Harem are still slaves under the control of eunuchs.

She also told me how the Kizlar Aghasi was reckoned to be the Sultan's closest confidant: the one person with whom the he could intimately discuss the behaviour and performance of both his concubines and his Ministers. On ceremonial occasions the unusual black face of the Kizlar Aghasi, traditionally just an uneducated former slave himself, is seen riding immediately behind the Royal Princes themselves, the sons and brothers of the Sultan.

The present Sultan, I learned, was so terrified of being assassinated that he trusted his black eunuchs in a way that he never trusted any normal man. They and the Kizlar Aghasi in particular in return made it their business to interpret and carry out his most secret wishes - including the killing of anyone the Sultan suspected of plotting against him or of wanting to introduce reforms and progress. Of course the very word progress was also anathema to the palace eunuchs, for their whole existence depended on the survival of the outmoded harem system.

Jane's just never going to believe what I'm going to tell her when I return to England.

Chapter 15 - Cut

It was next day and a mystified but terrified Jane was back in the tiled bathroom, tied down kneeling on all fours on a couch. Her head was held down, her legs fastened wide apart and a raised bar under her belly kept her bottom up high in the air. She was blindfolded and had no idea what was going to be done to her.

Suddenly she heard the falsetto voice of the black man who had so shamefully inspected her the evening before. He was talking and laughing in Turkish with Fazileh-hanum. The voices came towards from behind. Her intimacies, she realised with a blush, would be on view only too well to the dreadful man.

Horrified, she felt a hand between her legs. It was running down her precious beauty lips and parting them. She felt his finger on her clitoris. She tried to wriggle away but could not move an inch.

'Yes, very nicely fastened down,' Agha Ali said, 'now we can get on with preparing her so that her virginity remains intact for the All-Powerful.'

He opened a black bag, like a doctor's and handed the woman several forceps and a couple of shiny surgical clippers. 'Put these in boiling water,' he said, 'and sterilise them. It's something I was taught to do by one of the European doctors here in Constantinople.'

He laughed.

'And meanwhile we can have a little coffee, whilst your Negresses get the girl ready for her little operation.'

'Would you like me give her the same drug to dull her senses as we give to other girls?' asked the woman, adding with as laugh,

'Though they don't have the honour of being operated on by an Agha Effendi from the Imperial Harem.'

'No, I don't think that will be necessary and I like her clitoris to respond well to a little expert titillation before it is snipped off. In that way we snip off just enough to prevent any further arousal being possible without harming her. But I think we might have her gagged so that she not disturb us as we perform the operation.'

Jane heard Fazileh-hanum give an order to the two women. She was then gagged with a long cloth that was pushed into her mouth and tied behind her neck. What, she wondered terrified, was going to be done to her?

She was aware of a cold, freezing liquid being wiped over her displayed intimacies. In fact a few minutes later Agha Ali's hands again came between her legs and she felt his hot breath as he bent over her. Once again he parted her beauty lips, but this time forceps held them wider apart. He again tickled her clitoris until the bud became swollen and aroused. He nodded smiling as he heard the girl giving little moans of pleasure.

'I think this young lady has been used to giving herself pleasure,' he laughed. 'Well, she won't be able to do that in future.'

He slipped a small elastic band over the tiny bud, further engorging it and making it stand out. He stroked the firm little clitoris. The girl was again moaning with pleasure.

He picked up one of the surgical clippers with his now rubber covered hands. Very carefully he fitted the tip of her clitoris into the jaws of the clippers and then squeezed. The girl gave a little jerk and a cry of pain as she lost the sensitive tip.

There was a small and momentary spurt of blood, which stopped as soon as Agha Ali deftly poured a few drops of something that looked like Stockholm Tar onto the little wound.

'In two days it will have healed over,' he said, 'and the tar will fall off just leaving a tiny scar where once was her clitoris. Meanwhile we don't want her interfering with it - and anyway her virginity must be protected to ensure that nothing untoward happens to that before she is presented to the Sultan to be kept for deflowering. We don't want anything piercing what will be the privilege of the manhood of the Caliph, God's Lieutenant of Earth, to take, do we?'

Slowly Jane felt the pain easing. There was a strange feeling between her legs. It was as if she had lost something, but she had no idea what.

Her blindfold was removed. She saw the hideous black man closing a little black bag. He held something shiny in his hand. It was a small triangular shaped piece of silver chainmail, with chains fastened to the corners. Helpless to interfere with what he was doing, she blushed yet again as he deftly fitted the chain mail over her intimacies. Then, passing one of the chains up between her still outstretched legs, he joined it in the small of her back to the other two chains now coming back across her hips and locked all three together with a little padlock.

He came round in front of Jane and bent down to feel the tightness of the chainmail. He tried unsuccessfully to insert his finger under the edge of the silver mesh that was now guarding her virginity. Satisfied, he stood up and Jane saw him pocket the key of the padlock that she could feel in the small of her back. He then again went behind her and poured a little sealing wax onto the keyhole of the padlock, and sealed it with his large gold signet ring.

Jane's ankles were untied and her wrists released. Glancing in the mirror again, she saw the silver chainmail chastity belt locked round her waist. She realised that she was now no longer in control of her own body. And the key was held by this terrifying huge Negro!

Fazileh-hanum told Jane to put on her harem clothes again and led her back to her little room. Here the woman embarrassingly and explicitly showed Jane how, thanks to the open mesh work of the silver chainmail and the small size of the chain that went up between her legs, she could still perform her natural functions.

It would take a little practice, Fazileh-hanum humiliatingly told Jane, and then added that she would also have to keep the intricate silver mesh and its supporting rear chain spotless.

Chapter 16 - Helen Learns Yet More

16th May
I'm never tired of asking Maria's old nursemaid about the life behind the high walls that surrounded the harems of the various modern palaces.

I learned that even if a girl rises to the heights of being the First, Second, Third or Fourth Kadin, usually the mothers of the Sultan's sons, she still remains a slave and a member of her original Orta - and is still subject to the discipline of the Agha commanding her Orta. There is great rivalry between the Ortas to provide both girls for his bed and sons to succeed him.

'But there are compensation for the Kadins,' the Negress explained. 'At least they can be properly dressed. For the Kadins and other senior ladies of the harem are allowed to dress in the latest European fashions.'

'Oh yes,' interjected Maria, 'I've often seen them, veiled and guarded, of course, by black eunuchs, visiting the most expensive French dress shops in Pera. You often see them, being driven round the town in open palace carriages, beautifully dressed in the latest Parisian fashions and just wearing quite thin silken yashmak veils that sit on their noses and only just cover the bottom half of their faces. But they are always accompanied by angry black eunuchs armed with whips to make sure no man dares to look at them... Poor things!'

17th May

It all seems so extraordinary. On the face of it, life here in Constantinople with its well dressed men and women is all very civilised, and not all that different I suppose from life in say Paris or Vienna - or even Venice with its serenading gondoliers, or Cambridge with its punts and May Balls.

It's not only the European expatriate communities that I've met. I've also been introduced to many Beys and Pashas of the Ottoman ruling class. I was astonished to find that some of these were highly civilised Christians: Greeks, Armenians or from the Balkan provinces of the Ottoman Empire. Even the Moslems amongst them, Turks, Arabs, Kurds and Albanians, were also charming and well educated men who spoke fluent French. They wore European dress and were well read. They had travelled all over Europe. They appreciated Italian opera, Russian ballet and English theatre.

I've also met the wives of some of these leading Moslems. They might lightly veil their face with a silk scarf in public but they were intelligent women, dressed in the height of the latest Belle Époque fashions from Paris.

And yet apparently it was still considered quite normal for their husbands to follow the tradition of also keeping a bevy of beautiful white slavegirls shut away in their harems under the control of strict black eunuchs.

I can't wait to tell Jane all about it

18th May

This diary seems to be becoming more and more about harems. Well, the fact is that I'm secretly finding these conversations with Maria's former nursemaid about harem life, and then recording them here in this secret diary, to be more and more exciting. Yesterday evening when Maria's old nursemaid came to help us get ready for dinner, I could not help asking where all the women sleep in the harem.

I learned that they just sleep on Turkish sleeping mats on the floor, cooped up in the dormitory of their Orta and watched over all night by a patrolling black eunuch whip in hand to make sure they don't secretly try and use their fingers to play with each other - something that is strictly forbidden in a Moslem harem, where a girl's only source of pleasure must be her Master. I blushed remembering how Jane and I had so excitingly played with each other.

The Negress said that the eunuchs call it being unfaithful to their Master and are very strict about it. Woe betide any girl seen to put her hands below the bed clothes - and even worse if she is found under them with another girl, or even just alone in a room with another girl. The black eunuchs always suspect the worst!

'You mean,' I cried, blushing with embarrassment, 'that these... awful men... actually watch the girls the whole time to... to make sure they aren't... But that's terrible!'

The Negress explained how the black eunuchs feel that they are protecting the honour of the Master. It's a punishable offence for a girl not to make sure always that one of her supervising eunuchs can see her at all times - never mind being actually caught... misbehaving.

Apparently all the black eunuchs carry bamboo canes as a sign of their authority - and, don't hesitate to use them to punish the girls for the slightest thing. The Negress said that the eunuchs get a savage pleasure in caning women. It's really the only pleasure that they can enjoy and is a way of getting their revenge for the loss of their manhood.

Then I asked about what I had assumed to be the four pampered Kadins.

The Negress explained with a toothy grin that the Kadins have lovely private rooms over-looking the Bosphorus. Each room is differently decorated and has a beautiful extra big soft bed specially imported from Vienna and big enough to hold the Kadin and the pretty young concubines that the Agha of their Orta attaches to each of them to try and catch the eye of the Sultan.

'All in bed together?' I asked shocked.

'Oh yes, except when the Sultan is taking the virginity of a girl, the black eunuchs always like to provide him with several girls - made to work together to give him greater pleasure.'

'But isn't the Kadin jealous of these other younger girls?' I asked.

'Oh yes!' laughed the Negress. 'But she just has to bite her lips and put up with them. Jealousy is rampant throughout the harem. If it wasn't for the constant presence of the black eunuchs they'd all be scratching each other's eyes out.'

'Oh, so they're never really free,' I said.

'But what Turkish woman is?' interjected Maria, contemptuously. 'Except, of course, the sisters and daughters of a Sultan.'

There was a pause in the conversation and then I asked: 'But what happens to the others? Surely they aren't just drowned in Bosphorus these days?'

'One European girl was!'

'What!' I cried. 'I don't believe you.'

'It's true,' said Maria. Apparently she was caught by the Kizlar Aghasi having an affair with the Sultan's own teenage son. He was banished, but she was drowned in the traditional way.

The old nursemaid told us that some the older girls used to be kept on as Kalfas, or Mistresses. It was they who, with the black eunuchs, taught the girls how to please their Master the Sultan. But after the death of the Sultan Valideh, the Sultan's mother, some years ago the Kizlar Aghasi got rid of them, preferring the girls to be taught by the eunuchs of each Orta.

Goodness, I thought, how humiliating and yet exciting to be taught how to please the Sultan. And by a eunuch! How horrible!

Chapter 17 - Jane Meets the Sultan's Other Virgins

For two whole days, Jane remained locked in her room. All the time she was aware of the chastity belt locked round her waist. She could not get out of her mind that its key was held by that fat horrible black man, nor that it was he and not the women who had checked first her virginity and then the smoothness of her mound and beauty lips. Just who was this terrifying man dressed as a high Turkish official?

The memory of the terrifying whip was also still fresh in her mind. She kept asking her abductor what was going to happen to her and why the Negro had locked the belt onto her. But the woman would merely smile enigmatically and rub her hands together like a fishwife anticipating a profitable deal.

Every day a young girl would come and expertly wash and brush her long hair and then, under her abductor's supervision, would make up her face in the over-painted Turkish manner. Then she would paint her nipples to match her now painted mouth. Oh, how shame making! But she to admit as she secretly admired herself in the mirror that they had transformed her into beautiful young Eastern houri, with huge eyes ringed in black kohl and scarlet nipples glinting erotically through her transparent blouse.

Then Jane was made to practice walking round the room with her head up, her breasts swaying provocatively under her thin blouse, her hips swinging and an entrancing smile on her face - radiating a happiness which she was far from really feeling.

Several times a day she was brought delicious Turkish titbits and fruit. Jane wondered if she was being fattened up - but for what?

On the third day, Agha Ali returned. Again to her horror Jane saw that he was carrying his little black bag. Jane was held firmly by Fazileh-hanum as he unlocked Jane chain mail belt, parted her beauty lips and felt where once had been Jane's clitoris. Delighted, he pointed to a little healed scar.

'Good!' he exclaimed. 'Now I can sew her up, ready to be put into the Court of Innocent Virgins.'

'But she's already been cut,' objected Fazileh-hanum.

'Ah,' replied a laughing Agha Ali, 'but even if they have been, to make her feel all the more helpless as she awaits her deflowering by the Sultan, the Agha of the Innocent Virgins still likes to keep each girl also sewn up until the Sultan finally chooses her to be deflowered - as a change from his normal way of enjoying a young woman: up her bottom or in her mouth.'

The blushing Jane was then tied down on a couch with her ankles raised and wide apart. She was blindfolded. She felt a cold liquid being rubbed over her beauty lips, and then a series of pricks as Agha Ali expertly sewed her outer lips tightly together - but not so tightly as to prevent her natural wastes from slipping out between the laces.

Then she was untied. She cried out in horror as she looked in a mirror and saw her now laced up beauty lips with a little Imperial seal hanging down between her legs.

Agha Ali and Fazileh-hanum laughed delightedly.

'I'll send for her tomorrow morning,' he said.

They left the room leaving Jane scratching in vain at the laces and realising that under them she could feel nothing.

Next morning Fazileh-hanum came into the room carrying a silken rope. Before Jane could say or do anything, her hands had been securely tied behind her back.

Then the awful woman undressed and washed her. Then after making up her face and painting her nipples, she put Jane into a simple caftan over which she threw a long black shapeless cloak, a tcherchaf, that completely covered her from her hair to her feet with an oval cutaway for her face. But even this was hidden under a yashmak veil that covered Jane's face right up to her eyes.

Then, gripping Jane firmly by the arm, she took her again down the corridor. But this time she took Jane right out of the building in which she had been kept locked up for so long and pushed her into special little carriage that seemed to have been sent specially for her. A crest surmounted by a crown was painted on the door.

To her surprise two young black youths, dressed just as Agha Ali had been in black European morning coats, also got into the little carriage with her and locked the doors. She saw that in the left hand lapels of their coats gleamed the same blue crest as she had seen on Agha Ali's coat but that in their right hand lapels was a golden

Arabic number. They silently pulled down the blinds. She could not now see out at all. She would not see the dreaded Fazileh-hanum again.

The carriage moved off at a smart trot. One of the black men put a finger to his lips.

'You not talk!' he said in guttural French. 'You understand?'

Jane noticed that his voice was strangely high-pitched - again just like that of the terrifying Agha Ali. Was he, too a eunuch?

The carriage continued on what seemed to be a long journey whilst the two youths laughed and chatted in Turkish, glancing occasionally at the silent veiled figure of Jane sitting helpless between them, her hands fastened behind her back under her tcherchaf. Jane found herself dozing off as the carriage apparently began to be pulled up a long hill.

Suddenly it stopped and the two youths climbed, pulling Jane out behind them - walking awkwardly, under her shroud, thanks to her hands still being fastened behind her back. Peering through her veil, she realised she was in a beautiful park with undulating lawns dropping down to the sea and to what she would later learn was the Bosphorus and beyond that the hills of Asia. Cleverly placed belts of cedar trees split up the perspectives, but it was the numerous palaces in the park that made her really catch her breath. They were all painted a brilliant white, each with white marble steps leading up to an elaborate entrance, gleaming in the bright sunlight. Never had she suspected that her horrible jail had been so close to such marvels.

The youths seemed pleased with Jane's gasp of astonishment.

'Now you see, palace of His Highness. This Yildiz Palace, the Pavilions of the Stars - good name for palace full of beautiful creatures like you.'

His Highness! Did that mean that she, an innocent young English girl, who only a few weeks before had still been a schoolgirl in a convent, had been bought for the harem of the Sultan of Turkey?

Jane saw that the park was surrounded by a high wall and that the windows of the beautiful white palace to which she was being led were all covered by elaborate trellis work that made it impossible to see in. But she wondered, was it also to prevent anyone inside from escaping? Indeed, she wondered, what went on behind these covered windows and the beautiful trellis work?

'Look, girl,' said the other black youth. 'This one of the wonders of world. All people of True Faith contribute towards the cost of building new palace for Commander of the Faithful. This your new home as slave in the in the service of His Highness.'

'No!' cried Jane. 'I'm a free woman! I'm not a slave!'

'Oh yes you are,' laughed one of the youths, 'and we now in charge of you.'

'And,' cut in the other, 'and if we ever hear you speak like that again, we report you to Agha Ali for impudence. He thrash you - for impudence he give twenty strokes of his cane.'

Jane's brief revolt collapsed at these words which reminded her of her position. Tears filled her eyes as she felt herself gripped by the strong hands of her captors.

Peering through her veil as they came round the corner of a building, Jane saw numerous Turkish-looking men in black Stambouline coats or elaborate military uniforms, hurrying to other buildings or just strolling in the park. There were also veiled women, hidden like her under black shapeless dresses. Desperately she wondered whether to rush up one of them and ask him to rescue her. They might even know Maria's family - where Helen might still be!

But the firm grip on her arm was tightened.

'You not think any of these men would help you,' muttered one of the youths.

'No one, not even a European, will dare to interfere with a slave intended for the Sultan,' said the other, 'and you'd just get real thrashing.'

Jane's heart sank. Was there really no escape?

They arrived at a large isolated building surrounded by beds of brightly coloured tulips in flower.

'This harem,' explained one of the youths with a cruel laugh, 'your future home.'

Jane bit her lips in despair.

At a barred door, guarded by huge Black Guards carrying drawn scimitars, they were greeted by Agha Ali. Jane blushed under her thick veil at the memory of what he had done to her - and of the key that he carried. He was now carrying, like a sign of office, a long thin silver tipped bamboo cane with a curved handle.

'You be very polite to Mr Agha Ali,' whispered one of the youths with a nasty little laugh. 'He in charge of all girls in blue or Balkan

Orta - and he quick to use his cane on girls who not show him utmost respect.'

Scared, Jane gave a little bow to the horrible Negro. All this talk of him being in charge of girls! And a black man at that! And his cane! The very idea of being caned by a man made her tremble and blush! How awful! But what was even more awful was that despite herself, she could feel herself becoming wet with excitement under the silver chain mail that held her beauty lips tightly pressed together.

The last time this happened was with Helen on that day of term. Oh, where was Helen?

The big black man unlocked a solid-looking door and led the way down a corridor to an iron barred gateway. Jane could hear women's voices, but the only person she could see was another black man, also dressed in a Stambouline and also carrying a silver tipped cane. Glancing at the shrouded figure of Jane, he greeted Ali. He was clearly Agha Ali's equal. He unlocked a door and gestured to Jane to enter.

The room was large and cool and furnished in what Jane was to get to know as the Turkish style, with several big sofas and large leather cushions and Persian rugs. The walls were covered in a mosaic of coloured tiles. Through the windows, covered by bars and the strong looking trellis-work that she had seen from outside, could be seen the park and a distant view down to the Bosphorus, glittering in the bright sunlight: so near and yet so far.

An open alcove led to a tiled bathroom with a huge large bath in the centre - big enough to take several girls at a time.

A French window led out to a pretty sunlit white painted courtyard. Jane had a glimpse of flowers and a fountain which was playing in a pool, surrounded by tiles on which rugs had been placed. The pool and the rugs were completely shaded from the sun by an awning - Jane would learn that this was to keep the girl's skins white.

High up along the corner of one wall was a line of wooden lattice-work grilles. Evidently, she realised with a little shiver, they would enable someone to look down unseen into both the room and the bathroom - and into the courtyard.

Jane gasped as peering through her veil she made out three girls splashing in the shaded pool, their clothes neatly piled by the pool.

They were stark naked - except for wide shiny metal collar round their necks and an black leather manacles on heir wrists that were joined by a short length of equally shiny, solid-looking chain.

Two other girls, one wearing blue harem pantaloons and the other cream coloured ones, were kneeling up on their heels on the rugs, gossiping and playing with some dolls like little girls, occasionally peering into the room to see what was going on. The pantaloons were slung low on their hips, leaving their bellies bare. They too were collared and manacled.

They wore open matching boleros made of a stiff material that disclosed their painted nipples. On the sides of their heads were perched small embroidered caps of the same colour as their boleros and pantaloons. On their feet were little Turkish slippers with up-turned toes.

Three of the girls, including two in the pool, had a strange little distinctive white ribbon fastened to their collars. Jane in her innocence wondered what on earth that could signify.

Behind them in the shadows stood a young Negro, dressed in a Stambouline and carrying a long bamboo cane. It was like that carried by the two Aghas except that whereas theirs were silver tipped, his was only brass tipped. He was watching the girls.

Jane blushed as, watched by the two Aghas, the two black youths now took off her tcherchaf and yashmak and then her caftan. She was now stark naked with her hands still tied behind her back.

But worse was to follow for at that moment another very portly black figure entered the room. He too was dressed in a black Stambouline morning coat but the badge of office in his button hole was of gold, as was the gleaming tip of his cane. He was the Kizlar Aghasi, come to enforce his proud boast that no girl ever entered the bed of the All-Highest without him first having had a good look at her - to make sure she was worthy of the honour.

He was greeted with respect by the Aghas who pointed to the naked Jane as the latest recruit to the Court of Innocent Virgins.

To Jane's further embarrassment, Agha Ali took her by the arm and proceeded to show her off to his colleagues, both whom ran their hands in turn over her body, smiling enthusiastically as they did so. They were both clearly impressed by the pretty Jane with her long honey-coloured hair, her blue eyes, slim waist and long slender legs. But they seemed even more impressed by her firm and yet full young breasts, which they kept lifting up and weighing with their experienced hands as they congratulated Agha Ali on his purchase.

'I think His Highness will enjoy looking down at this one as she awaits her deflowering,' the Kizlar Aghasi said to Agha Ali with a wink - pointing up at the grille in the wall.

'Yes,' added Agha Vazid, 'he usually likes to take one innocent virgin every week, as a change from the well-trained concubines and Kadins. So I like to keep at least half a dozen from different Ortas here for him to choose from.'

He turned to Agha Ali. 'But you will remember how he recently deflowered three of your Romanian virgins from in as many days and this seriously reduced my stock. So this new English virgin of yours will be very welcome to help keep up the numbers.'

The three senior black eunuchs, who were talking in Turkish and periodically pointing to Jane, were evidently discussing her. She would have been even more embarrassed had she known that they were now discussing her monthly cycle and deciding when she too would next be ready to wear the mysterious white ribbon round her neck. Unknown to her, it indicated to the watching Sultan that there was little or no chance of her then conceiving by her Master. This was of course a key consideration for the eunuchs - for they were responsible that the Imperial succession was not upset by the unexpected arrival of new white progeny.

Meanwhile one of the youths had picked up a high shiny collar similar to that worn by the other girls.

'His Highness like see slavegirls wearing his collar,' he said, pointing to the Imperial crest engraved on the side of it. 'And this your harem number.' He indicated a line of Arabic numerals.

He put the collar round her neck and closed it shut forever with a click. But with her hands still tied behind her back there was nothing she could do to stop him.

Then Jane saw that the other youth was carrying some blue coloured silken clothes.

'Now we dress you as slavegirl of our Blue Orta,' he said, as he made her step into blue transparent pantaloons. Then he slipped a blue stiff, shamefully open, bolero over her shoulders. These were followed by a little blue cap and Turkish slippers.

But the youths had not finished with her. Deftly they painted her exposed nipples scarlet and her mouth too, outlined her eyes with black kohl and brushed her long hair down her back. They dropped a little belladonna into her eyes, making her pupils huge. Finally, unfastening her hands and bringing them, to her relief, round to the front of her body, they locked soft leather manacles joined by a two foot length of shiny chain onto her wrists.

They stood back to admire their work and pointed to a long mirror. It showed a strange, chained and half naked blond girl, dressed and made up like an Eastern houri.

'You now in Court of the Innocent Virgins, awaiting like other girls your deflowering by the Sultan at a time of the month when the Agha says you will not conceive.'

Court of the Innocent Virgins... awaiting your deflowering by the Sultan... belong to Blue Orta... time of the month... not conceive. The words raced round Jane's brain. She blushed at such talk, not quite sure if she knew what they meant. Her convent upbringing had been very strict.

'But' he added, 'you always remember that you belong to Agha Ali's Blue Orta. As can see, there's another girl from our Blue Orta also here awaiting deflowering.'

The other youth then thrust a very pretty doll into her hands. 'You not allowed books here, but His Highness likes see virgins playing with dolls like innocent little girls.'

'I now leave you in care of my friend Agha Vazid,' said Agha Ali, leaving room with his two youthful assistants. He was followed by the Kizlar Aghasi, satisfied that that the very pretty Jane with her slim but buxom figure would satisfy the Sultan's requirements.

Vazid led the half-naked Jane out into the courtyard, clutching her doll. He gestured to her to kneel down between the other two girls. 'No, not kneel cross-legged like a man,' he said, admonishingly raising his silver tipped cane. 'Slavegirls always kneel legs apart.'

Then he turned away to speak to the young eunuch standing in the shadows. As he was pointing to Jane, she realised he was briefing his assistant on her.

Putting down their dolls, the two young girls took Jane's hands sympathetically.

'You must be the new English girl we've been expecting,' whispered one of them in quite good French. 'Welcome to the Fish Pond.'

'Fish Pond?'

'That's what we call it. We're just like the fish are kept in fish restaurants. They never know when they're going to be suddenly taken out and cooked, so we never know when we are going to be taken out and "deflowered"... whatever that really means... by our unknown Master.'

Jane shuddered.

'I'm Mina,' said the girl dressed, or rather half-dressed, in blue. 'I come from Bulgaria and like you I'm in that horrible Agha Ali's Blue or Balkan Orta.'

'And I'm Djovane,' said the other girl. 'I'm from Circassia and I'm in the White Circassian Orta.'

Jane told them her name.

'Jane!' cried Mina, 'What pretty name. And you're pretty, very pretty.'

Jane saw that they, too, were very pretty: Djovane with long blond hair and Mina with dark hair. Both had huge dark eyes and big sensual lips. Both were wearing the same revealing harem costume as herself, nipples painted the same scarlet as their mouths, beauty lips sewn up with strong black laces just like Jane's.

'We Christian slavegirls - virgins like you.'

'And like you,' she said pointing up at the grille, 'waiting like all the girls here to be chosen by the Sultan whom we have never seen. We never know when. We don't even know when he is looking down at us to size us up. Nor do we know just what will happen when we are chosen - for the girls chosen never return here and we never see the other girls in the harem who have already been "deflowered".'

Like most respectable English girls of the period and like her equally innocent companions here, Jane had no real idea of what went on in the marriage bed - something which, for the Sultan, made his collection of innocent virgins all the more entrancing.

Mina laughed with a flash of her black eyes. 'Here, if you've big breasts like yours, you're lucky. Maybe the Sultan will choose you soon.'

Chapter 18 - Helen Has Some Exciting News

19th May

Oh, I'm so excited! Earlier today Maria rushed into my room to say that we've all been invited by the Sultan to a ball at the Dolmabahcheh Palace.

'But what shall I wear?' was my first reaction. My two existing ball gowns were well and truly aired by now.

But Maria told me not to worry. Her wonderful kind father was so delighted to be invited that he says we can both go and buy new dresses from Maison Worth, the best Parisian dress shop in town. They have some gorgeous dresses. I'm going to look the Belle of the Ball!

And when we ran into David Lyons at a the Tennis Club this afternoon he said he was going too with the Senior Officer of the British Naval Mission here. How wonderful!

21st May

For the last two days, Maria and I have been could think of nothing except the forthcoming ball.

Dresses and delicate little shoes have been tried on and discarded and then tried on again. Our hair has been dressed in one style after another before the perfect one was decided on. Numerous different make-ups and expensive French scents were tried out and discarded and finally selected.

Oh, it's all so exciting - and just in time before I have to go back to dull old England again. Oh sad it is that Jane isn't here too, she'd have loved it so.

Chapter 19 - Excitement Also in the Court Of Innocent Virgins

But the Mavroyeni household was not the only one excited by the prospect of the Ball. The Sultan had announced that he was moving down to the Dolmabahcheh Palace with the harem, which had been electrified by the news. It would be an exciting if frustrating event for the secluded Christian slavegirls, even if they were only allowed to watch the Ball hidden behind the screens specially built high up into the walls of the huge Throne Room.

The excitement even spread to the more isolated girls of the Court of Innocent Virgins, for the Sultan made it known that he would also be taking them to the Dolmabahcheh Palace. He liked to have them on hand, ready for one to be taken whenever the mood took him.

Moreover, to protect their innocence, there were also special quarters for them in the Dolmabahcheh, isolated as in the Yildiz Palace from the rest of the harem. There was even a specially isolated screen through which they could watch whatever was going on in the Throne Room, not only without being seen or able to call down, but also unable to talk to the other girls in the harem - who had already lost their virginity to the still very virile and lustful Sultan.

So it was that Jane found herself looking wistfully through barred and screened windows at the ships ploughing up and down the Bosphorus and bound for the Black Sea or Mediterranean ports of Europe - and freedom. Freedom! Would she ever be free again now, she kept wondering - like her companions.

Even more poignant was the sight of European Ambassadors and their staff arriving by boat at the steps almost below her window for an audience with the Sultan. On one such occasion, her heart beat violently as she saw the Union Jack flying proudly from the bows of the British Ambassador's smart looking steam pinnace, crewed by sailors from the British naval guard ship.

Indeed on his occasion the Agha had, smiling, let her beat her hands in vain again the thick glass windows as she screamed to the unhearing Ambassador: 'Help me! Help me! I'm an English girl!'

Desperate to attract his attention and quite unable to do so, she saw the Ambassador resplendent in his diplomatic uniform, being greeted by the Sultan's equerries and led away into the far end of the palace.

The Agha smiled again as, watched with sympathy by her companions, she fell to her knees in an impotent rage, beating the floor with her puny manacled fists and sobbing: 'Oh it's not fair, it's just not fair.'

It did not, he reflected, do any harm for a virgin to be made to realise that she was now just a helpless slave.

Chapter 20 - Helen is Entranced

Helen's heart was in her mouth as the Mavroyeni carriage took its turn in the long queue to sweep proudly through the high and imposing outer gateway that led on into the formal French-style gardens of the palace.

The gateway had been built in the Ottoman baroque style with a mass of carved urns, rosettes and garlands - like a triumphal arch. It was clearly intended to outdo anything at Versailles or Sans Souci in Berlin.

Turkish soldiers in smart new uniforms lined the way in and a band played the rousing Hamidiye march, which had been specially composed for the Sultan.

As the carriage swept up to the steps of the palace entrance, Helen caught a glimpse of a strangely high wall cutting off part of the garden at far end of the palace. It seemed almost a hundred feet high, with no footholds and nothing at the top. It looked quite unscalable. Was the harem behind those walls? Goodness!

Handsome young Aides-de-Camp and Equerries, the golden cords of their aiguillettes glistening on their right shoulders showing they were in the service of the Sultan himself, respectfully handed Madame Mavroyeni and the two girls down from the carriage.

One of them seemed particularly attentive to Helen and as he gave her hand a little hidden squeeze, he mentioned his name: 'Ayab Bey. At your service Mademoiselle,' her murmured obsequiously. Helen blushed and then blushed again as he added in an even lower voice. 'Mademoiselle is indeed lovely!'

Ayab Bey! It was a name that she would have reason to remember.

They swept into a large reception room decorated in the latest Victorian and Troisième Empire styles from London and Paris with numerous satin covered chairs and sofas.

Then, after giving their wraps to attendants, they moved into a huge hall with on either side a beautifully designed double flying staircase with red crystal banisters. The staircases seemed to be suspended as if by magic in mid air and they both led up to yet more large open reception areas. A huge crystal chandelier lit up by hundreds of candles hung down sparkling between the two facing staircases.

'A present from your Queen Victoria,' whispered Maria. 'They say it weighs ten tons and it was sent here without a single one of the ten thousand pieces of glass being broken.'

Helen thought that she had never seen anything so grand - or so ostentatious.

They joined the guests circulating around the two large open reception rooms at the head of the two staircases and along the balconies that joined them. The large rooms were filled with huge gilded mirrors, porcelain fireplaces and crystal torchieres rising six feet from the marble floor.

Black servants dressed immaculately in the red livery of the Sultan were offering Champagne and the most delicious Turkish and French canapés on huge silver trays. Were they eunuchs, Helen wondered? She looked at their smiling but hard faces. Previously she had imagined that eunuchs, black or white, would be rather weak, pitiful and vacillating creatures. But there seemed nothing weak or pitiful about these determined looking servants.

Suddenly a large and portly black man swept through the room. His bearing and self confidence were impressive. He was wearing the black double breasted Stambouline of a high official. He looked cruel and cold.

'The Kizlar Aghasi!' whispered Maria.

The Sultan's chief black eunuch. Goodness! Horrified she saw that he was indeed carrying a slim gold tipped wand like an emblem of office, just as Maria's old nursemaid had described. She remembered what the Negress had told her about the eunuchs enjoying using their canes. My God, had this one just come from beating a young white slavegirl? The mere thought made her feel dizzy.

With the Kizlar Aghasi was another large but slightly younger and slimmer Negro.

'That's Agha Ali,' whispered Maria, 'a very senior black eunuch. They say he might be the next Kizlar Aghasi and that he has earned the special favour of the Sultan by providing him with a stream of fresh white slavegirls.'

Fresh white slavegirls! The very words made Helen blush.

Clearly impressed by Helen's blond beauty, this second eunuch paused as her passed her. He bowed, but as he did so he looked her up and down with a professional eye.

Helen and Maria drifted over to the windows of the large reception room. From there the view across the Bosphorus through the numerous high French windows was sensational. No wonder the previous Sultan had chosen this place to build a new palace to replace the old, rambling, dark, medieval Topkapi palace in the old part of the city.

She looked down at the white marble of the Sultan's landing stage. It was lit up by flaming torches held aloft by eunuchs. She watched as the leading dignitaries of the Ottoman Empire and members of the Diplomatic Corps all stepped out of their highly polished kayiks, resplendent in their gold embroidered European style diplomatic or military uniforms and often accompanied by unveiled ladies dressed like herself in long bejewelled ball dresses. Oh, their jewellery! Oh, their diamond necklaces and sparking earrings! It all made her feel quite sick with jealousy.

Chapter 21 - Helen is Noticed

Helen saw Maria's father beckoning to her. He was talking to a man dressed in the uniform of the Sultan's advisers. With him was the young equerry who had been so attentive when she arrived.

'This is Hussein Pasha. His Excellency is one of the Imperial Majesty's most intimate advisers,' Maria's father said to Helen, 'and Ayab Bey is one of His Highness's equerries.'

Helen curtseyed to them both. Then turning to the Pasha, Maria's father added: 'Mademoiselle Helen Hamilton is from England - a school friend of my daughter. She will shortly be returning to England on the Orient Express.'

The Pasha bowed. 'Such beauty should not be kept in the cold of an English school,' he laughed.

'Oh no, Your Excellency,' replied Helen naively, 'I've left school. I'm on my own now!'

It was a remark that made Ayab Bey stiffen.

Just then Maria's father was called away by a friend.

'But surely your parents...?' asked the Pasha.

'Alas, Sir, they are dead.

Again Ayab Bey stiffened. 'Well,' he said, 'we must find a way of tempting you back soon to Constantinople!'

'That would be lovely. There is nothing in the world I would want more,' Helen heard herself saying fervently. 'And it wasn't as though I had anything to go back to in dull old England.'

Was it, she wondered, the Champagne speaking, the atmosphere here or the thought of the nearby shut up slavegirls? Or rather was it perhaps the presence of David Lyons, dressed in his smart naval Ball Dress, whom she had just noticed looking at her admiringly from across the crowded room.

'And I'm sure,' she added, 'that my guardian would only too keen to rid of me. But once back in England I suspect he'd say he couldn't afford to send me back here again - and I couldn't possibly impose on the Mavroyenis again - kind and hospitable that they have been.'

The Pasha and the young equerry exchanged looks.

'It is indeed a pity that you have to leave so soon,' the Pasha murmured with a smile, 'especially if you have nothing to go back to.'

He turned to the young equerry. 'His Highness would have would have enjoyed meeting her. He likes the English.'

'Perhaps, that can be arranged,' said Ayab Bey enigmatically, as Maria's father returned to take Helen off to meet another friend.

Chapter 22 - The Throne Room

The sound of music wafted through from the centre of the huge palace. The crowd began to go down the two staircases, the women holding out their long spreading dresses. Helen saw that that everyone was making their way through the large open halls to an imposing archway.

She caught her breath as they entered the towering Throne Room. Fifty Corinthian columns supported an exuberant *trompe l'œil* ceiling a hundred and fifty feet above them. It was frescoed like the backdrop for an Italian opera with pillars, clouds, curtains and garlands of flowers. High up in a balcony covered in gold leaf, the Sultan's Italian orchestra was playing the latest waltzes from Paris and Vienna and down below couples were dancing.

Maria caught Helen's arm and pointed to a raised canopy facing, across the vast room, the French widows that looked out onto the Bosphorus. There on a priceless carpet stood the gold imperial throne of the Ottomans, transported here from the Gate of Felicity in the old Topkapi palace.

Surrounded by a bevy of Beys and Pashas in diplomatic uniforms and a huge black man dressed in a Stambouline, sat a small saturnine figure in a tailcoat emblazoned with the stars of orders and with a wide blue silk ribbon across his chest. It was the Sultan himself! The man whose photograph appeared everywhere in Constantinople.

She saw that he was watching the dancing attentively, his quick half closed eyes going from one couple to another. Was he comparing the low cut dresses of his female guests with the bare bosoms of his slavegirls next door in his harem?

She saw that leaning over his shoulder was Ayab Bey. He seemed to be pointing her out. Suddenly the Sultan's hooded eyes lit upon her. Helen felt quite weak.

Just then her arm was taken. It was David. Politely, he asked Maria's father if he might dance with Jane. She saw that the Sultan's eye was still on her as they made their way to the dance floor.

Then as she relaxed in David's strong arms, she saw something glistening from behind a long line of screens screen high up above the French windows that looked out into the Bosphorus. She could make out vague shadows moving behind them.

With a gasp, she remembered what Maria had said about the ladies of the harem being allowed to watch the Ball from behind a screen. My God, there they were! This wasn't just some fairy tale made up by Maria's old nurse. This was for real!

Chapter 23 - Another View of the Ball

Kneeling down on a line of cushions alongside several other concubines, Jane was peering enviously down at the ball through the screen. She and the other Innocent Virgins had been given special permission by their Agha to go and watch it from their secluded room. It was like a box at a London Theatre, except that there was a lattice work screen across the front of it, through which they could see without being seen.

Mina explained that each of the Ortas had its own similar box.

Agha Vazid and his young assistant were seated at opposite sides of the room, making sure that their charges behaved. They were still carrying their canes.

Jane sighed. The sight of free European women in their lovely ball dresses, dancing in the arms of handsome men, made a sharp contrast with her own skimpy harem dress - and her clinking manacles. It was a scene that highlighted the way the eunuchs prevented the harem girls from having any such contact with any handsome young men - or indeed any man except their Master and his horrible eunuchs.

Her Master! Yes, the cruel vicious looking figure sitting on the throne was her unknown Master. Her owner. She looked at him with increasing hatred.

It was just then that Agha Ali slipped into the box to see how the two Innocent Virgins from his Orta were getting on. Quietly he watched Jane and Mina.

Jane saw a smartly uniformed young man leaning over the Sultan and apparently pointing to a dancing couple: a good-looking young man in naval uniform and a beautiful and rather English-looking girl with dark lustrous eyes. There was something very familiar about the girl.

Jane gave a sudden gasp. It was Helen! Helen was here! At the Ball - and dancing with a handsome young naval officer. Oh, it was too much. She must contact her. She must show her where she was. She must tell her what had happened to her. Then Helen's friends would get her out of this awful harem.

'Helen!' she called out. 'Helen! Darling!'

Vainly she called out and beat on the metal grille trying to attract Helen's attention. It was hopeless.

Agha Ali had seen her reaction. He had also seen the young woman whose attention she had vainly been trying to attract. How interesting, he thought. Perhaps here was another little bird to be entrapped. Another English girl! He must hurry down to the Ball and speak to the Kizlar Aghasi.

Epilogue - The New Gedekli

It was a few days later and, as the Orient Express pulled slowly out of the station in the evening light, Helen was sadly waving goodbye to Maria and her parents - and to David Lyons who had also come to say goodbye - or rather *au revoir*, for they were both determined to see each other again back in England.

Then, as the train followed the line of the Bosphorus as it widened into the Sea of Marmora, she settled down in her first class carriage which, rather to her surprise, was empty. Back to London, oh how sad! But at least she might be able to see Jane again. Goodness, she had so much to tell her.

She was still mulling over what she was going to say to Jane when the train made an unscheduled stop at a remote wayside halt out in the country - on the orders of a young military officer. In Turkey no one ever questioned the military. It was now dark.

Ayab Bey came to the door of Jane's compartment. Behind him was a file of armed soldiers, keeping everyone back. The astonished Helen recognised him from Ball. Politely he explained that he had orders to escort her back to Constantinople where the Sultan was anxious to discuss with her the sending of his children to school in England. She should not worry, however, as she would be put onto the next train and her guardian in England informed by telegram.

No one saw Helen as wonderingly, but feeling very flattered by the Sultan's request, she stepped down from the train. No one saw her as the train resumed its journey and as Ayab Bey politely handed her into a closed carriage - a carriage in which Agha Ali and the two young assistant eunuchs with whom he had collected Jane, were was sitting awaiting her.

But in the hand of one of the youths was a pad soaked in chloroform. As Helen stepped into the carriage the other youth seized her hands whilst his colleague held the chloroform pad to her mouth and nose.

No one ever knew what had happened to her. Her guardian, highly relieved by her disappearance which meant that he would not now have to account to anyone for his misappropriation of her money, gladly accepted the explanation that she must have been killed when falling from the train somewhere in the wilds of the Balkans.

When Helen awoke she found she was immured in the Imperial Harem, the latest recruit to the Sultan's team of Gedekli, his Maids of Honour.

CONTINUED IN BOOK TWO

Printed in Great Britain
by Amazon